Amazon Swamp Victory

Treasure Rebels Adventure Novella, Volume 3

Gerard Doris

Published by Gerard Doris, 2023.

AMAZON SWAMP VICTORY

First edition. September 27, 2023.

Copyright © 2023 Gerard Doris.

ISBN: 979-8223065937

Written by Gerard Doris.

Also by Gerard Doris

Treasure Rebels Adventure Novella
Nile River Scorpion
Congo Spider Fangs
Amazon Swamp Victory
India Yeti Pirates
Greek Gladiator Sharks

Standalone
Wrath of the Renegades

Watch for more at https://gerarddoristhrillers.com.

Table of Contents

PART I: ELECTRIFIED RHINO

(Amazon Rainforest – South America)

The shocking roar of a black jaguar echoed from behind a wall of fog. After a few quiet moments the jungle predator unleashed another cry warning all other male challengers to stay away from its territory. Slowly the giant cat padded across an immense tree limb hanging thirty feet above the ground, until it stepped clear of the blanket of fog which concealed the tree tops. It then paused and looked down at the slow moving waters of the Amazon River a hundred feet away, then at the tree line along the riverbank for prey to eat.

Suddenly the quiet was shattered by another howl, this one from a challenger below who wanted to enter the jaguar's hunting ground. The black cat opened its mouth revealing two rows of jagged white serrated teeth, and lifted its head back to reply with a menacing howl of its own.

But it stopped, closed its jaws and looked up as a new and strange sound filled the sky. Ten seconds later the outline of an Embraer Phenom 300 private jet appeared out of the clouds, the South American sunlight flashing brightly against the painted silver green fuselage. Suddenly scared the jaguar turned and disappeared back into the wall of fog while its rival below had already run for cover amidst the shrubs lining the river.

The plane continued its slow descent, flying a hundred feet over the muddy brown water of the famous river until banking right and cutting across the tops of the fog covered trees. The fog seemed to evaporate for a couple seconds and a clearing atop a large hill suddenly came into view. Expertly the Phenom's pilot coasted down onto the grass covered hill, and the multimillion small plane slowly rolled to a smooth stop eighty feet from the edge, where far below the Amazon Rainforest stretched out in every direction. The pilot finally cut the engines and as the roar of the jets slowly faded away a quiet stillness followed...until the air-stairs suddenly clicked open and lowered to the grass with a metallic hiss.

Immediately on the hill three armed mercenaries dressed in black military fatigues slowly walked forward to wait at the bottom of the stairs. Behind them parked in a semi-circle were two black enormous reinforced SUV's known as Rhino's, two small ATV'S, and one green all terrain Brutus Motorcycle, a small machete and radio tied securely to its side. They had been waiting impatiently for two long hours for the Phenom 300 to land.

Ted Claymire was the first person to disembark. He was six feet tall, had dyed brown hair that had been shaved almost completely off, was fortyish, and had piercing brown eyes that somehow seemed hostile and afraid all at the same time.

His t-shirt almost ripped with every movement due to his unusually large chest and 21 inch biceps. He prided himself on being a "world class athlete," but his stiff rigid movements and unnatural body shape revealed he was little more than a steroid monster. But while he had resorted to unnatural methods to attain strength, he had naturally inherited a high level of intelligence. During the last twenty years he had accumulated over five university degrees specializing in history and engineering, built a thriving company, and had trained in the vain hope of becoming an Olympian one day.

Behind him was his thirty year old sister, Sharen Claymire. She had the fluid graceful movements and natural attractiveness of a high end fashion model, but today her blond hair was pulled back in a tight ponytail and almost every inch of skin covered by layers of jungle fatigues. Despite her humorous attempt at preventing mosquito bites, her insistence on still wearing perfume endlessly attracted jungle bugs to her face.

Unlike her brother she wasn't brilliant, and had resorted to using charm and seduction to try to climb the ladder of power in society. But to her frustration most men ignored her, claiming that despite her obvious beauty, they found her unnerving and creepy. She brushed the criticism off and stated that it was the strange eye colour she had inherited from her father that was the problem. But it wasn't the colour of her eyes but the eerie emptiness behind them that caused most men to run the other way.

Realizing that her seductive charms were ineffective she turned to her brother for financial support. Together they built a criminal business which specialized in the selling of "hot" antiquities which had been stolen across the planet.

Their father furiously rejected their new "business" plans and begged them to quit, but they instead only grew more obsessed with the corrupt money they were making. When their father finally threatened to disown them they promised to walk away from it all...until they found out who their grandfather had been and the special treasure he had left behind. Since then they had travelled the world trying to discover where he had worked, operated, and lived over fifty years before. A near impossible task as the "Bounty Hunter" had specialized in leaving almost no trail behind.

They never did find his final resting place or even an old photo of his face. But they did learn that the treasure lay in South America hidden in the mysterious depths of an Amazon swamp.

No longer concerned about their father's threat they assembled a mercenary team and located the secluded swamp...only to discover that the swamp harboured more danger than they could have imagined. Horrified they realized that they would need outside help, that only the best in the world would be able to survive a dive into those mysterious eerie waters.

That meant kidnapping the Treasure Rebels.

Ted and Sharen both reached the bottom of the stairs and stepped onto the wild jungle grass, stretching their arms as they tried to get rid of the irritating feeling of jetlag. They nodded a greeting to their men and turned around to look back up at the air-stairs as the Treasure Rebels walked down towards them.

The first was twenty-something Maddox Tarver, the leader of the group. Wearing unique copper tinted sunglasses and sporting spiky blond hair, he looked more like an athlete from the X-Games than a famous treasure hunter and scuba diver. His relaxed almost aloof manner suggested someone used to living a life full of boredom, when in reality he had experienced and pursued more adventure than most could in multiple lifetimes.

Behind him was Travis Jagson, a thirty-year old Hawaiian and former heavy weight boxer. Travis had given up the chance to become a world champion to instead accept Maddox's offer to become a Treasure Rebel roughly two years prior. Like Ted his biceps and triceps were as large as some people's legs, but unlike Ted he was still athletic and had built every muscle through natural hard work.

Behind Travis was the last member of the team, twenty-seven year old red haired Amber Monette. Like Travis she had walked away from a famous career, hers being an astrophysicist at NASA, to join Maddox and become a globe-trotting treasure hunter. Like Sharen she had the physique of a supermodel, but the similarities stopped there. Unlike Sharen whose eyes were dead looking and empty, Amber's were wild, warm, and full of life.

All three were wearing the same jungle fatigues they had worn in the Congo a week before, minus their knives and other tools. Even Amber's high tech tablet was locked away in one of the jet's cabinets.

With the mercenaries training their guns on them they walked up to the Claymires who were resting against the black hood of one of the reinforced Rhinos. Behind the Rebels three more armed mercs which included the pilot climbed down the air-stairs as well onto the hilltop. One of the men was carrying a large brown box whose top was taped over with duct tape.

With everyone now gathered around him, Ted opened a ragged looking dog-eared map and laid it across the hood as he pulled out a red marker and began scribbling on it.

"Okay, Tarver, this is where we are right now. The swamp lies two miles north of here down there in the jungle. We'll take the Rhino's and ATV's down this path until we reach the Amazon River. From that spot it will be another hour's drive through the jungle path until we reach the isolated swamp. All three of you understand?"

Travis stood impassively with his arms crossed and replied, "We've known the coordinates since you told us a week ago in Africa. We're still waiting for you to explain what little trinket we're to pull up out of the swamp goo."

Ted grinned and folding up the map nodded to the man holding the brown box. The mercenary immediately placed it onto the Rhino's hood where Sharen tore the duct tape off and pulled out a true size replica of a 1950's era diver helmet covered in gold, jewels, and diamonds. Despite being made completely of cheap tin, every artificial nut, bolt, jewel, and diamond appeared real, even the gold coloured paint. There was even a sheet of transparent plastic placed inside to duplicate the glass faceplate.

As the replica was passed around Ted continued speaking, "Our grandfather as you know was a bounty hunter in his day, the very best in the world. He captured fugitives and resistance fighters during the war, and anyone else he was hired to catch. He was a true professional."

Travis spit on the ground in disgust and interrupted him, "The Bounty Hunter was a sicko gutless monster."

Ted paused, rattled that anyone would say that of his grandfather and after a speechless couple seconds he decided to ignore Travis and continued, "He was a legend. Not a single man ever escaped him, and he amassed a small fortune for his excellent work. My sister and I are aware you have been following the trail of our grandfather's closest ally, the German genius Wolfgang. We want you three to know we don't care about him, or whatever reason it was his grandson attacked you. In fact we thank you for putting him in jail, he stole an important map of the Congo from us months ago. So please understand, we do not hold a grudge against any of you; we simply want your help to retrieve the real helmet in the swamp."

Travis grimaced and looked at Maddox and Amber. "If we find their little trinket for them they won't kill us. What kind-hearted gentle people!"

Ted disregarded Travis' mockery while Sharen continued the story in her chillingly cold and strange voice, "Back in the 50's our grandfather had a famous fight with the one man who had eluded him for over a decade. This man was wanted in multiple countries and was finally captured here in the Amazon. Our Grandfather then chartered a steamboat to take him and the prisoner out of the jungle but something terrible happened...the prisoner broke out."

Amber interrupted, already tired of the Claymires' history lesson, "I don't understand. You both are professional divers, have a large team, and access to the best equipment in the world. Salvaging and searching the swamp should be easy."

Ted responded irately, "We tried. We failed. And we lost our best divers."

Sharen quickly explained, "The swamp is exceptionally dangerous. We sent three divers in and not one of them ever resurfaced. We suspect the swamp is full of freshwater Bull Sharks."

Travis grinned at Ted. "Why don't you go in and give it a try?"

"I did...after what I saw I'm not going back."

Amber handed the replica to Travis and asked, "How big were the sharks you saw?"

"I didn't see one. What I saw was a ghost. A ghost diver."

Silence filled the air for a full five seconds until Amber replied with a small hint of sarcasm, "You're afraid of ghosts?"

Ted's face flushed red with anger but before he could respond Sharen practically yelled, "My brother and I *ARE NOT* superstitious. But what my brother saw had to be a ghost."

Travis was also grinning, unbelieving their claim. "Why?"

"The ghost was wearing dive equipment over half a century old."

"But there was no cord extending out of the water, or anyone else to be seen on shore." Sharen added.

Behind them Maddox had stopped listening, and was instead staring out into the distance and down at the open jungle below. His face was expressionless, but behind the copper tinted sunglasses his eyes were full of intense surprise at what he saw. Travis and Amber noticed their friend slowly stepping away from the bulky vehicle and towards the Brutus motorcycle.

"So you think your men were killed by this...diver ghost?"

"My men were killed by some freshwater predator, Jagson. We pulled their remains out of the swamp. Some fish clearly bit right through their dive suits and limbs. We-"

Maddox took off and ran through the ring of mercenaries towards the Brutus motorcycle.

"Get him!"

The next second Travis' fist drilled straight into the side of Ted's jawbone and the thief's body flew backwards landing heavily into the dirt. Instantaneously Amber pushed Sharen, sending the crook sliding across the vehicles' hood until she crashed onto the ground, her strange eyes bursting with shock.

Amber and Travis then jumped through the open windows on each side of the Rhino, and Travis shifted gear and hit the accelerator. The SUV roared and the specialized wheels churned across the thick grass towards the hill path which led down towards the jungle. Two seconds passed before any of the surprised six man squad reacted.

"The wheels!"

Machine guns fired and the Rhino's back wheels were instantly shredded. The black SUV spun crazily to the right. Travis gripped the wheel and tried to regain control as the supersized vehicle slid madly for thirty feet, until it slowly tipped and crashed on its side, the back wheels still spinning as the smoking torn rubber continued to fly off the rims and into the air.

They lifted their arms in surrender and climbed out through the driver's side, uninjured but covered in glass from the now cracked windshield and seething at their failed escape attempt. But the moment they stepped back into daylight they smiled.

The Brutus motorcycle was gone.

Maddox was free.

==================

Maddox pushed the throttle as far as he safely could and the Brutus rocketed down the jungle path, finally reaching the bottom of the hill and disappearing beneath the rainforest canopy as he entered the fog shrouded jungle.

He spun the wheels left without hesitation and pushed the Brutus forward through a small clearing. He had never been to the mighty Amazon before. But he knew exactly where he was heading.

He had to hunch over the handlebars to prevent being thrown off by the low hanging tree limbs and more than one branch sliced across his face. The path suddenly seemed to end as a mass of thick tree limbs stretched down almost to the ground.

Maddox slid the bike sideways underneath the jungle covering, and the Brutus slid forward for twenty feet before he righted the bike now clear of the tree limbs. He was now at the edge of a small clearing. To his right a dozen yards away came the quiet sounds of water flowing and an unknown animal screech. The Amazon River.

Then he froze when he saw the faces.

Peeking out from behind a row of trees cloaked in fog were over twenty painted faces of a native tribe, their faces covered in red, black, and blue natural dye. It was the first time Maddox had ever met an indigenous tribe and he wondered why they had painted their faces in such bright colours. A quiet moment passed as a man from the modern world, and a group of men whose way of life hadn't changed for hundreds of years, stared at one another in surprise and a little fear.

Maddox then looked up and spotted patches of smoke rising above the trees roughly a mile away. He then heard the oncoming roar of the other Rhino and the two ATV's. He pushed the throttle and the bike roared down a small gully then up the other side and back onto another dirt path as the natives watched with awe. Then in an instant they had disappeared back into the fog.

In ten seconds the Rhino appeared tearing through the jungle growth and followed behind by the ATV's. The driver was experienced and he immediately spotted the Brutus' track leading into the gully. He shifted gear and the black Rhino leaped forward into the gully, leaving behind a swirling cloud of muddy dirt behind its wheels. In two seconds it had reached the top edge and with the V8 engine screaming the Rhino leapt out of the gully, crashed down onto the new ten foot wide path, then accelerated again.

As the ATV'S churned up the mud and followed behind, the Rhino driver turned on his bright lights to gain a better view in the darkened path where little sunlight shone through the trees overhead. His lights immediately lit up the green motorcycle two hundred yards away and with a little smirk the driver pressed the accelerator even further.

Maddox could hear the roar and knew his enemies were closing in. The path suddenly swerved to the right and Maddox adjusted his speed and expertly turned into the curve, jumping thirty feet clear of the ground before landing safely back onto the path. Despite the seriousness of the situation he couldn't help but smile. He had never driven a bike as amazing as this.

The thick tree branches above finally thinned out and the daylight shone down. Now able to fully see he increased the Brutus' speed even more, while behind him the Rhino reached the hairpin curve and slid thirty feet before its back end crashed into the trees. A couple seconds later both ATV riders foolishly took the curve without safely slowing down, and they both lost their balance, overturning and smashing into the side of the pinned Rhino. One rider was tossed towards the dirt path where he rolled to a stop with a grotesque looking broken ankle, while the other rider clipped the Rhino's bumper and with a yell he felt his shoulder tear out of its socket. As both riders briefly screamed in painful agony, the other three mercenaries inside the Rhino jumped out, lifted their comrades into the back seats, and together pushed the pinned SUV out of the trees. Leaving the twisted remains of the two wrecked ATV's behind they then continued the chase.

Far ahead Maddox approached the end of the path which ended in a T. He quickly turned left and followed this new path which twisted uphill. The moment he reached the top he knew he had made a mistake. He was trapped. Impenetrable jungle blocked every way forward...except for a steep rocky slope that led fifty feet downward and ended in a precipice which hung forty feet over a body of water. Maddox revved the bike and swung close to the edge to look down.

It was a mysterious looking swamp, less than a hundred yards in length and width, with the occasional odd looking tree branch sticking out of the dark coloured water. Off to one side was a decrepit looking wooden pier, and across the water on the opposite side rings of smoke could be seen rising above the trees from the jungle beyond. He smiled for an instant. He was looking at the famous swamp where the treasured helmet had vanished decades before.

He then heard the roar of the Rhino as it climbed the hill towards him. He only had two options. One was to surrender and likely be killed by the Claymires later. The other was to try a stunt only a handful of men in the world could survive. Luckily Maddox was one of those men.

Just as the black SUV appeared he pushed the throttle and the Brutus plunged over the edge and tore down the slope towards the swamp below. The Rhino immediately followed, its front wheels spinning as it half slid down the rocky face behind him.

The Brutus reached the end in seconds and Maddox timed the jump perfectly. The all-terrain motorcycle leapt off and began to soar across the open swamp.

Up above the Rhino's driver smashed on the brakes the moment Maddox flew off the precipice. He had never guessed Maddox's intention and had thought the treasure hunter was trapped. He pressed the brakes as hard as he could, even pulling the emergency brake in a panicky attempt to stop the multi-ton machine in time.

But the Rhino was going too fast, was too heavy, and the angle was too steep.

As Maddox let go of the motorcycle at the right moment and began to drop towards the swamp below, the Rhino flew off the edge behind him, the men inside jumping clear into empty space as well.

For two long seconds it felt as if time had slowed down as Maddox, the five men, the motorcycle and SUV with wheels spinning flew through the air before dropping into the swamp with a furious series of splashes that echoed for miles into the jungle.

Maddox was the first to resurface, spitting the foul tasting water out of his mouth. A moment later the five men began to poke their heads clear of the swamp's surface as well, some laughing disbelievingly that they had survived. They then began to swim for the wooden pier while Maddox swam in the opposite direction. Fifty feet away the SUV was slowly drifting, already half sunk.

Suddenly two large black tails appeared out of the water in front of the swimming mercenaries, twisting in the air before slapping the swamp's surface and disappearing again beneath the darkened water. Maddox heard the men yell in panic and turning he saw the tails just before they glided below the water. He could only guess what creatures they were, and with renewed strength he swam even faster for shore.

Unexpectedly one of the men began shaking as if he was being electrocuted, and in seconds he was pulled under. His associates swam over to help him until the water's surface was broken by the face of a hideous looking electric eel, two feet wide in size and covered in mud and grime.

The men panicked and turned frantically back, followed by both eels which began to circle the men and the slowly descending SUV.

Maddox continued to swim in the other direction, his arms pulling him through the water at an incredible speed. As the swamp's edge grew close he could see out of his eye the Brutus motorcycle's front wheel barely sticking out of the brownish green water in the distance...and then it finally sank below the surface for good.

The four remaining men climbed up onto the sinking Rhino, yelling in fear and throwing what they could at the fifteen foot long eels which were circling them. One of the men pulled out a handgun and fired multiple rounds into the water. Every bullet missed. Suddenly one of the massive creatures leaped out of the water, its body slamming against the side of the SUV. Instantly the creature sent well over a thousand volts of electricity coursing into the Rhino's steel. All of the men were killed instantly, dropping lifelessly into the water. The gargantuan sized eel then twisted back in the air away from the steel SUV before tumbling into the water with a splash, moments before the Rhino completely sank from view as well.

Stunned at what he just witnessed, Maddox turned away and finally reached the swamp's edge where an enormous thirty foot tree grew out of the shore, its thick branches drooping down onto the water's surface. He reached up with one hand and grasped the closest branch and tested its strength. The branch held. He then seized the limb with both hands and hauled himself up, covered in mud and algae.

Halfway free of the swamp his momentum suddenly stopped. Something below the water had grabbed his leg. He immediately suspected one of the eels had bitten into his boot, and he spontaneously tensed for the inevitable electric jolt that would destroy him.

But the heart stopping shock never came.

Instead the creature below kept pulling Maddox down towards the depths of the swamp, and Maddox was dragged back down into the water up to his neck. He hit back, lifting his other leg and kicking down with everything he had. He expected the boot's heel to smash into the soft tissue of the eel's head, but instead he felt the boot break through something hard, and he could hear a subdued *crunch* sound from beneath the water.

Whatever it was, the creature immediately let go and he reached back up for the tree branch.

But to his horror he suddenly felt the creature grasp his leg once more, and despite Maddox fighting with every ounce of courage possible, the leader of the Treasure Rebels was finally pulled under.

PART II: SWAMP GHOSTS

(2 hours later)

The second Rhino slowly came to a stop in the mud beside the quiet swamp. The Claymires, Travis, Amber, and the single surviving mercenary climbed out and stared at the swamp's still surface.

Sharen repeatedly tried the radio but no response ever came. The last transmission the Claymires heard from one of their men was that the Rhino was sliding out of control towards the water, and then screams before the radio signal went dead.

Beside them Travis and Amber quietly waited, both wearing their own specialized scuba dive suits including their trademark underwater chainsaws. After kidnapping the Treasure Rebels in the Congo the Claymires had allowed them to bring their own dive equipment, storing it all in the Phenom 300's cargo compartment for the long plane ride. But apart from the chainsaws, dive suits, and small dive knives strapped to their legs, Amber and Travis were not allowed to bring any other piece of their own equipment down to the water. With most of their men missing, the Claymires had also asserted that only the bare essentials be driven down to the swamp, insisting that Amber's computer tablet and even the replica dive helmet made of tin were to remain on the plane.

Everyone stood quietly at the water's edge for another long moment, the Claymires worrying that they might not be able to finish the mission if their men were dead. While Travis and Amber worried they would never again see their good friend.

But their concern passed swiftly, because deep down they instinctively felt that Maddox was alive. They had heard the last frenzied transmission from Sharen's radio hours before as well, and if the Claymires' men had been in trouble it probably meant that Maddox had outwitted them.

Travis had enough of the long wait and glared at Ted.

"It's about time you told us what scares you so much down there."

Ted pulled out a pair of binoculars and while examining the swamp spoke, "What I saw was real Jagson. An ancient looking diver from long ago, he was wearing the full brown wetsuit, the old helmet, even the oxygen cord. A ghost diver. You know how I know he was a ghost? When I drew close I saw inside the helmet through the glass...there was nothing to see, no face, only dark emptiness!"

Travis and Amber listened intently, still confident Ted must be wrong but nevertheless growing slightly uneasy.

"Perhaps some of Wolfgang Jr.'s contacts arrived here ahead of you. He beat you to the Congo, maybe he beat you to the Amazon as well."

Sharen shook her head pompously at Amber, "You're wrong! Wolfgang *never* knew of the treasure helmet, and this is one of the remotest parts of the Amazon. We are alone out here."

"Maddox and your men might still be alive."

Ted finally turned away from the water to face Amber and Travis, "They're all likely dead. Including Mr. Tarver. You can bring his body up...after the treasure."

Sickened and tired of being in the company of amoral criminals, Amber walked away and climbed up onto the wooden pier. Travis instead waited to make one last request.

"We need more than chainsaws and small knives to survive down there. I'm not afraid of your loopy ghost story Ted. I am concerned about Bull Sharks. We each need a weapon or tool to keep predators a good distance away if need be. Think Ted, if we die, you have no chance of ever findin' your little treasure."

Ted hesitated then snapped his fingers at the lone mercenary who had been training a machine gun on both Treasure Rebels ever since they parked on the swamp shore.

"Get the blue crate!"

The merc nodded and handed the gun to his boss, then jogged to the back of the SUV and pulled out a plywood crate with blue lettering stamped across the top. He set the crate down into the black mud, pried open the lid and pulled out a spear-gun used for hunting fish. He then exchanged the underwater "gun" for the machine gun with his boss.

The unnaturally shaped thief then turned to Travis. "You only get one long distance weapon, not two."

He then promptly handed the spear-gun to Travis, his face twisted in a strange sneer.

"Remember Mr. Jagson...treasure first."

Travis stared back and wished he could drive another vicious right hook into Ted's face and wipe that ugly sneer away. He instead spit into the swamp with utter disgust and walked away, climbing up onto the timber pier beside Amber.

Now together they slowly walked to the edge while securing their dive masks, speaking to one another through the mask intercoms.

"You ready to prove these two are just as stupid as their grandfather was?"

Amber grinned for the first time in hours, her turquoise eyes behind the dive mask full of enthusiasm.

"Of course Travis!"

Now ready to face anything they jumped in together.

Immediately they turned on their dive mask lights and the rims of their goggles filled with clear white light. Swimming side by side they descended and took in the unusual sight before them.

The swamp water was surprisingly clear beneath the green algae above, and while visibility was only about eight feet, it was over fifty with their lights at max power. They reached the bottom and Amber looked at the digital display in the lens of her mask which included the swamp water temperature and her oxygen tank level.

"All systems in the suit working."

"Mine are workin' perfect too."

They slowly swam forward until Amber suddenly pointed into the gloom ahead.

"Maddox's bike!"

Travis turned to look and saw the Brutus thirty feet away resting in the swamp mud. The back half of the bike was already submerged in the swamp goo while the front wheel, handlebars, and part of the seat still remained clear of the mud. But there was no sign of the machete or radio.

Instinctively they swam towards it.

But they froze as one of the fifteen foot eels suddenly swam out of the darkness above the mud, its body twisting side to side as it glided smoothly through the water. It circled the

Brutus twice then curled around the bike's seat and began nibbling on one of the protruding handle bars.

"It looks like an electric eel!"

"I didn't think they could grow past ten feet!!"

Travis turned and through the gloom fifty feet away he saw his dive mask lights reflect off something metallic or chrome.

"I think the SUV is over to our left."

"Lead the way Travis!"

Happy to leave the eel behind as it continued to chew on the sunken motorcycle, they swam swiftly towards the chrome reflection until their lights lit up the smashed remains of the Rhino.

The wheels had already disappeared into the swamp muck and the windshield was broken into a million cracked pieces. Even underwater the horrible dent from the ATV crashing into the passenger side rear door could be seen.

Suddenly Travis held up his hand and pointed into the gloom beyond the vehicle. "Hold up! Did you see that?"

Amber nodded her head as two more creatures with dark scales briefly passed into their mask light range before swimming away.

"Black Caiman. Ten feet long. Part of the alligator family."

They waited until they were certain the alligator-like caiman were out of range, then their attention went back to the sunken SUV. They split up to circle the vehicle, carefully looking inside without touching anything. What they saw wasn't pretty.

"There's blood in the backseat."

"A lot of blood in the front too," Travis responded sombrely.

Amber then slowly kicked her long slender legs and swam to the back where the trunk window was cracked like an elaborate spider web. She paused, struggling to see through the fractured glass.

BAM!

The glass *exploded* as an eel's head smashed through the window directly in front of her! She tumbled backwards into the black mud as the electrified predator struggled to pull its head and body through the glass.

Travis heard her scream and immediately swum above the SUV until he looked down at the eel as it continued to shake free of the broken trunk window. He grasped the spear-gun, took aim, and fired from above.

The steel barb shot through the water directly into the eel's brain. After a couple violent death spasms it stopped moving for good.

Travis then swam down and pulled Amber free of the mud, making sure never to touch the Rhino in case the eel's body in its final moments had sent a jolt of electricity into the vehicle. Together they hurriedly swam away until the smashed frame of the Rhino and the dead eel disappeared into the distance.

Carefully scanning the water for any signs of a new predator, they took stock. While Travis studied the used spear-gun Amber wiped some of the mud off her legs and arms saying, "Where are the bodies of Ted's men...and what ate them?"

Travis replied without looking up, "Probably caiman food."

Amber wrinkled her face under the mask, "Disgusting but likely. I doubt that blood belonged to Maddox. His bike was too far away. I still think he made it out into the jungle."

"Me too."

Travis tossed the now empty spear-gun into the mud and said, "Let's go east and head away from the bike and Rhino."

They soon entered the very heart of the swamp. The minutes went by, and the only creatures which swam into their view were a handful of bright purple and red Discus fish, their orange eyes examining the two scuba divers with suspicion and almost humorous curiosity.

They continued forward in silence until an immense seven foot long fish with gray scales and a narrow head swam into view a few feet in front of them. The mammoth fish then gyrated in fear the moment it saw them, before whirling away into the swamp darkness for good.

Travis grinned and spoke through the intercom as they both realized it had only been a large freshwater fish. "Thought for a second that was the eel from the motorcycle!"

"I'd rather see that ghost Ted is afraid of than another eel!"

Ten seconds later Amber got her wish.

Out of the gloomy shadows their lights illuminated the ghostly looking outline of another diver thirty feet away. As they kicked closer they suddenly understood Ted's reaction.

The ghostly figure was wearing everything divers had worn over a half century before. They could see the gloves, boots, helmet, and greyish brown dive suit, and there really was a dive cord extending out of his back and leading away further into the swamp. Eerie red sparks were visible in the dark water as the "ghost" appeared to be using a cutting torch they had never seen before.

"I thought Ted was just some paranoid wuss."

Amber didn't respond. Her vocal cords seemed frozen in shock but her mind was still working. She double tapped a button on the side of the goggles and the digital camera within her mask began to take pictures of everything she was seeing.

Travis fought his initial reaction of wanting to head in the opposite direction and instead kicked his legs to move even closer. "C'mon pretty girl. Let's see what he's really doin.'"

"Let's dim the goggle lights Travis. We don't want who or what he is to see us."

"Copy that."

They each pushed another button on their masks and the bright white light from the goggle rims immediately dimmed to LOW POWER. Immediately the beams of light were cut to about ten feet of range.

But they didn't have to fear losing sight of the "ghost" diver, as the sparks flying around him were impossible to miss, and the light from the torch's flame reflected off the old looking dive helmet.

Slowly the two Treasure Rebels approached, carefully sweeping the swamp floor and perimeter around them with the lights as they grew close to the eerie looking figure.

When they were within ten feet they switched off the lights, Amber's mask still snapping multiple pictures every second. As they closed in the only sounds to break the ominous quiet were the strange hissing from the ghostly cutting torch and the thumping of their heartbeats pumping furiously beneath their dive suits.

The "ghost" was using the cutting torch to slowly cut a small 4x4 square through the rusted metal of an old steamship which lay on its side on the bottom of the swamp. The wild splay of sparks in every direction illuminated most of the overturned hull, and the dim reflection showed that the old steamboat's metal underside had already been cut into over a dozen times. Travis and Amber watched closely as the "ghost" expertly sliced through the metal with confidence, their specialized dive mask lenses protecting their eyes from the blinding torch light.

Up close the ghostly figure's strange equipment became fully visible. While the helmet, shoes, boots, and suit did appear to have a design from an era long ago, they could see a strange brown rubber covered everything, even the helmet. And the greyish suit was unusually bulky compared to navy divers from the 50's. Travis and Amber were experts in underwater technology, and the strange suit before them was unlike anything they had seen before.

"He looks like a cross between an old school navy diver and something out of a sci-fi flick!"

"The whole suit looks strange...as if the arms and legs have been insulated somehow," Amber replied.

Travis looked at the diver's unusual dive cord as it snaked away into the murky gloom.

"Let's see where the ol' dive cord goes!"

But as they turned away the dark water was lit up by four underwater beams of light...coming from four more ghostly divers who were approaching them from behind!

"Go up!!"

But as they turned to swim for the surface they saw two more divers also wearing the same strange equipment quickly descending down on top of them!

Blam!

The ghostly diver by the steamboat's hull suddenly reached out and seized Travis by the neck, the cutting torch now turned off and tied to his belt. Travis instinctively reached back and grabbed the diver's arms, trying to shake free, but the diver had an incredibly tight grip, and in seconds he had begun to pry Travis' mask off. With two powerful kicks Amber was beside them prepared to hit the diver in the face.

The "ghost" saw Amber coming and quickly kicked out, hitting her squarely in the knee and sending her spinning backwards to the side. But not before she had grabbed the torch off his belt.

As the team of mysterious divers quickly closed in above and around the rusted hull, Amber looked up and saw one of the approaching lights reflect off a dive knife attached to the ghostly looking diver's leg. With horror she saw the "ghost" rip off Travis' dive mask and pull the serrated blade out of its sheath to deliver the death blow.

She pulled herself up, reached forward, turned the cutting torch on, and in one motion brought the red destructive flame straight down onto the "ghost's" helmet.

A million orange sparks sizzled in every direction and the diver let go of Travis and turned frantically towards Amber.

For the first time she saw the old antique dive mask face to face, and she realized that Ted hadn't been lying. There was no face to see behind the glass, only blackness.

But the gurgled scream she heard came from no ghost, and the man inside turned away in a vicious panic and pulled a switch along his dive belt. The torch immediately lost its power for good and the man rushed away into the swamp gloom. The rest of his team closed in on the two Treasure Rebels.

In desperation Travis searched the swamp floor for his mask and half blind he finally grasped it covered in the swamp muck. He wiped the slime off the best he could and pushed it back down onto his head. The suit immediately beeped and the water inside was drained out. The digital readout on his mask before his eyes flashed green to signify the dive suit's system was fully operational, and to Travis' relief he felt oxygen being pumped back into the mask once again.

The six mysterious divers suddenly stopped approaching and paused as if they were sizing up the Treasure Rebels. Then as if they had been given an order, they each pulled out the same serrated dive knife attached to their legs and moved in for the kill.

Travis and Amber responded by pulling out the underwater chainsaws from behind their backs, pushing the red trigger buttons and slicing the spinning serrated teeth through the water in front of their new enemies. The six men immediately halted and a tense stalemate ensued, and the only sound to be heard underwater was the intimidating hum of the incredible chainsaws.

Suddenly a loud metallic **clang** echoed dully through the water from behind Amber. She quickly turned her head towards the corroded steel hull.

"MADDOX!!"

Ten feet away, sticking his head out from one of the cut openings in the steamboat's hull was the leader of the Treasure Rebels, waving his arms for his friends to follow him inside.

Travis and Amber immediately let go of the red triggers and as the chains whirred to a stop they swam furiously towards Maddox. The six divers clumsily tried to stop them, but their slow movements meant only the diver closest to Amber was able to block her path.

She quickly cut up and to the left, completely evading the criminal except for her right dive fin which accidentally brushed against the glass in the faceplate of his helmet. For a split second his view was completely obscured by the dark outline of the fin, and was immediately followed by the handle of Travis' chainsaw smashing into his face.

The handle cracked the glass in three places and the man immediately dropped the knife and began rushing to his accomplices for help, while Travis kicked his legs and propelled himself through the water in the opposite direction. In moments he had followed Amber inside the shadowy corroded hull.

They both reactivated their dive mask lights to FULL POWER and the broken insides of the ship lit up before them, including Maddox who was swimming ten feet ahead through the maze of crusted pipes, splintered rotted wood, and corroded mashed steel. Maddox reached the far side and with a powerful kick he left the ship's hull through another opening in the rusted steel, this one naturally made when the ship had crashed decades earlier. His friends followed seconds later, swimming through until their heads broke the surface.

Hot jungle sunlight poured down from above, revealing a small cave only about a hundred feet in diameter, surrounded by stone walls where rainforest trees could be seen swaying in the rainforest breeze forty feet above them. Resting against one of the rocky walls in the dirt was Maddox, still wearing his sunglasses while the machete and radio from the Brutus rested against the cave wall beside him. Around his neck was an old cord and a key that looked like it belonged in the Victorian era.

Amber turned her head and her dive mask light then lit up the only other object in the cave...another 1950's dive suit standing upright and covered in green algae. But unlike the suits worn by their attackers in the swamp, the cloth was torn and faded while the dive helmet rested atop on an angle, the faceplate open and cracked in four places. The suit was empty, except for a large hairy pregnant rat which had made a nest in the broken helmet.

Travis pulled off his mask and smiled as he climbed out of the water to stand before the suit. "I say we give the old helmet to Ted and Sharen with the rat included!"

"It's not the same helmet they're looking for."

Travis turned to look at Maddox who was now fidgeting with the Brutus' radio.

"It has to be it! I bet the jewels and diamonds were taken off and hidden somewhere in the suit."

Maddox opened the radio into two parts and answered while studying its components.

"The treasure helmet is somewhere in the underwater jail covered over by the ship's hull."

"How can you be sure?"

"I saw the clues in the Bounty Hunter's hideout in the Congo."

Amber climbed out of the water and sat down, pulling off her dive mask and letting her long red hair fall down across her shoulders.

"We worried you were dead!"

Maddox grinned for the first time in the cave, "I got pulled under by one of those dive goons. I broke his faceplate with a single kick but he still pulled me under."

Travis left the rotting suit and sat down beside his friends. "I'll bet he wondered how you could see underwater with those sunglasses on!"

"He couldn't see much with the glass cracked in the helmet, but no matter what I did I couldn't break free. Then suddenly one of those bonkers eels appeared, it actually began wrapping itself around his head! He immediately let me go, and I headed straight for the Brutus where I grabbed the radio and blade before heading for this hideout. I knew Ted and Sharen would force you two to dive anyway, and I've been swimming out every couple minutes through the steamboat's hull waiting to signal you. The goons in the retro dive suits ain't spotted me once."

"How did you know about this place?"

Maddox didn't answer, instead he angrily snapped the radio halves closed, frustrated he couldn't get it to work.

"I'll try it!" Amber proposed.

He quickly handed her the damaged radio. "You got it. Can it be fixed?"

She held the radio up into the sunlight and studied the damaged parts closely.

"Most likely Maddox!"

Travis rested his head back against the cold stones of the cave and asked another question, "Did any of Ted and Sharen's men make it out? We found the Rhino's interior covered in blood."

Maddox explained sombrely, "They're all dead. One of the electric eels sent a jolt of electricity through the SUV killing everyone. The only people now in the swamp are those weirdoes cuttin' into the steamboat. Did either of you get a close look at the suits?"

Amber looked up from the radio, "The suits appeared ancient but the sleeves, legs, and body looked as if the material was covered in some sort of rubber....I bet the suits are specially insulated to protect against electrocution."

Maddox kicked a clump of swamp slime off the bottom of one of his boots and responded, "The dive suits aren't the only thing that's unusual. Up close their helmets look strange; unlike anything I've read about or seen."

"I'm certain they're high end professional grade blended with new cutting edge technology. I wouldn't be surprised guys if those helmets cost more than all our gear combined."

"Maybe so, but I prefer our stuff any day."

"Me too."

She then opened a hidden compartment on her left shoulder and pulled out a case filled with small tools. She then chose a tool the size of a toothpick and began poking away at the radio.

"Well at least guys we know why Ted and Sharen have been so anxious. Someone just as dangerous as them is after that treasured helmet too."

Travis replied, "And now we know how Wolfgang beat us to the waterfall in the Congo. He stole the map from the incompetent Claymires!"

Travis then stared at the pool of water at their feet which led back into the swamp and wondered out loud, "I still don't get how the divers breathe. Where do their dive cords go? And how can Ted and Sharen have never once seen them entering the swamp?"

"I suspect the cords surface somewhere deep in the jungle. Over the last two hours I've seen over a half dozen men take turns cutting into the hull. Every time they arrive or leave it's from the same direction that's opposite the hill Ted and Sharen's plane landed on."

A dozen seconds of quiet then filled the cave until Travis pointed to the key around Maddox's neck. "Find that in the steamboat's hull?"

"It was tied around the waist of the old dive suit there."

"Have a hunch what it opens?"

"It opens the prison cell."

Travis didn't bother to ask how Maddox knew, instead he looked up at the jungle trees swaying in the wind high above through the cave opening. He then studied the rocky stones, boulders, and dirt which lined the cave walls.

"We'll have to climb out."

Maddox shook his head. "Already tried man."

Puzzled, Travis looked back at the opening far above then at the stony walls.

"You can climb twice that height in minutes!"

He then noticed the machete beside Maddox was streaked with blood.

"Animal?"

Maddox pointed at the severed carcasses of a couple small snakes littered across the cave dirt. "Small but highly poisonous. They're living amongst the rocks above our heads."

He then lifted one of his boots and rolled up his pant leg, showing multiple bites into the boot's heel.

"Good thing man I wore the reinforced boots or the fangs would have punctured right through!"

Amber suddenly stood and with a loud *snap* she closed the radio back together and tossed it to Maddox.

"Try it!"

He quickly began adjusting the radio's frequency while Travis looked at the old dive suit to his right, just as the hairy rat poked its head out and began sniffing a strand of green algae hanging across the glass.

"If that's not the helmet the Claymire's want, and it's not the fancy modern tech those ghostly goons are wearing out there...then who used this suit long ago?"

Maddox jumped to his feet and replied without explanation, "The old jungle man."

Travis and Amber looked at one another completely puzzled, never having heard the name before.

"THE WHO!?"

Maddox didn't respond to either of them, instead he continued focusing on the radio which had suddenly come to life with irritating static. Happily he looked at the others as he fine-tuned the signal.

"Let's see who we can reach!"

He quickly spoke into the microphone asking for emergency help.

But no security official responded.

Instead the dull static was suddenly broken as if the signal had been hijacked, and a moment later a strange threatening male voice resounded from the receiver and echoed throughout the cave.

"*TREASURE REBELS! MY NAME IS HECTOR BRAGARD, AND YOU HAVE ONE MINUTE TO BRING UP MY HELMET! I HAVE CAPTURED THE CLAYMIRE SIBLINGS AND THEIR PLANE. YOU HAVE NO WAY OF ESCAPE OUT OF THE SWAMP! COME TO THE SURFACE PEACEFULLY WITH MY HELMET, OR I SEND MY MEN INTO THE STEAMBOAT TO FIND AND KILL YOU!*"

Maddox looked coolly ahead, his eyes filled with fierce concentration behind the sunglasses as he thought on how to respond to this new enemy who had suddenly changed everything.

It only took one second for him to decide what to do.

He pushed the button and spoke.

"Go ahead man, send them in!"

PART III: THE OLD JUNGLE MAN

"We're trapped in here Maddox! We can only hide for so long in the ruins of that boat!"

Maddox grinned and tossed the phone back to Amber.

"It'll take them at least half an hour to search all the way through and reach this cave. We want them down there while we make our way up to the jungle."

Travis pointed at the machete.

"What about the snakes? You just said the wall is infested with them."

"Your special dive suits should be thick enough to prevent a bite through."

Travis slowly stood his face filled with uncertainty.

"But what about you?"

Maddox didn't respond immediately. Instead he walked over to the olden dive suit and grabbed the two strange, unusually thick, algae covered brown gloves that hadn't been worn in half a century.

"I'll have to hope these are thick enough!"

He then grabbed the machete and tied it to the cord around his neck, then swung the cord around so the key and blade were resting against his back. He then turned to his friends. "You two ready?"

Travis nodded he was ready and grasping his dive mask he closed it back atop his head, pressing another button in the mask which opened multiple air vents and disconnected the special mask from his oxygen tank. With another push of a button the heavy oxygen tank then dropped into the dark sand.

Amber opened the radio case again and pulled the inside components apart. "They better not be able to track us." She then reattached her mask and released her dive tank as Travis had, and together all three began climbing towards the green rainforest high above.

The first ten feet nothing happened. Then the next twenty passed without a sighting. Then suddenly it seemed as if all the snakes living in the rocky wall of stone had decided to slither out.

One snake recoiled then shot forward towards Travis' head. The Treasure Rebel instinctively turned his head away and the creature's fangs missed, biting into empty space beside his ear. Travis then grabbed the serpent with one hand and roughly pulled it out of its hiding place, tossing it down where it plopped with a small splash into the dark blue pool of water.

Amber had three strangely coloured snakes coil around her arm, then her mask. Unable to lose her grip she instead froze, unable to see anything through her mask lenses except for reptile skin. After ten anxiety filled seconds the three creatures slithered back into the wall crevice and she continued her climb upward.

Maddox was the least lucky. Four times he placed his hand into a crevice for support and felt the terrible pressure of a snake biting into the glove. Two more times when he placed his boot into a toehold, a pair of fangs leapt out and stabbed into the boots reinforced heel or toe. But never once did the snakes' venom filled teeth reach his skin, and Maddox kept climbing as if the deadly serpents weren't even there.

Five minutes later the Treasure Rebels reached the apex of the climb and with relief they clambered out of the cave and rolled onto the warm jungle grass.

Travis looked back down at the still empty pool of water. "No sign of Bragard's men yet."

He then sat upright and lifted his hand back to check that the chainsaw was still secure in the holster after the climb. But he froze as his fingers felt another snake slither around the chainsaw's red trigger, onto his hand, then onto his arm, then to his horror it slowly began to slither into his helmet! With a yell he undid the dive mask and in one motion he tore it off his head and hurled it, along with the snake, down into the cave far below.

A moment passed as all three looked at one another without speaking. The only sounds to be heard were the shrieks of howler monkeys watching them from above in the trees, and the faint sound of gurgling, bubbling, moving water.

Amber pulled off her dive mask and wiping a strand of red hair away from her eyes looked towards the sound.

"Is that the Amazon River?"

Maddox instead was looking at the tree tops above them and at a curling wave of smoke drifting upwards a half mile away.

Travis noticed and pointing at the smoke in the distance asked, "Is that why you took off with the motorcycle?"

Maddox stood and tossed the ancient gloves back down into the cave and nodded yes.

"Someone you know?"

"Someone who knew the *Rainforest Rogue*."

Travis and Amber looked at one another before replying together, "The old jungle man?"

=================

(Half-Hour Later – Amazon River)

Maddox, Travis, and Amber hastily ran the half mile through the dense jungle until they stood on the bank of the Amazon River, the emerald green plants, tree leaves, and sinewy pale coloured vines less than a couple feet above their heads. Roughly four thousand miles long, much of the Amazon River cuts through rainforest while thousands of species of fish and other underwater creatures call its flowing waters home, including piranha and anaconda snakes. While much of the natural world has been "tamed" by mankind, the mighty Amazon River is one of the last places on earth that still retains some mystery and wildness.

Travis pulled out a specialized small canteen from inside a shoulder pouch in the dive suit, and studying the greenish brown water as it flowed past he lifted the canteen up to drink. But before he could take a sip, a strange looking curved claw bent down and slowly pulled the canteen out of his hand. Startled, he looked up as a small and hairy tree sloth, hanging upside down and covered in tan coloured fur, slowly pulled itself up to another tree branch while holding onto the drink. Then with Travis yelling at it to stop the sloth slowly lifted the canteen to its mouth until all the water splashed out over its entire face.

As the small creature began shaking the now empty canteen for more to come out, Maddox and Amber burst out laughing while Travis gave up yelling and just waved his hand at the sloth indignantly.

"Okay you little freak you win."

The sloth didn't seem to understand; instead it slowly turned to Travis and smiled as only a sloth can. Then it stretched out its clawed hand incredibly slowly until the canteen was only a foot from Travis' face. He looked at the canteen, then at the mold and ant covered brown fur along the sloth's arm. He didn't want the canteen back.

"You keep it, you hairy little outlaw."

The diminutive sloth smiled even more and pulled the canteen away for good.

Amber continued laughing and chidingly said, "He's not a little freak Travis!"

Travis replied as he watched the sloth slowly crawl upwards until it finally disappeared into the upper branches.

"But he is a thief."

Following Maddox's lead all three then continued forward along the river bank, ever watchful of any caimans that might be resting in the grass or just watching the shore hidden from view in the water. They never saw any, but they did see two large male boars furiously fighting over a female, the loser finally being head butted straight into the river where it screeched in shock. Horrified the loser boar furiously kicked its small legs and moved through the water until it stumbled up onto the riverbank before a large predator could strike from beneath the river's surface.

At one point Amber spotted a group of small bearded Tamarin monkeys watching them walk past from behind a wall of shrubs and jungle flowers. Each of the small orange haired monkeys seemed nervous, except for the largest male of the group who sat calmly with one of his hands resting against his bearded chin. He looked as if he was lost deep in thought pondering the big questions of life.

Suddenly the jungle foliage along the river's shore thinned out, and their path led up a small twenty foot hill. As they climbed faint wisps of smoke curling into the blue sky could be seen rising from whatever lay below on the other side. As they ascended Travis asked Maddox, "How well do you know this old jungle guy?"

"More like he's heard a lot about me."

They stopped and looked down at a small campsite below, where the small remnants of the fire dimly crackled as a large pan rested above it containing cooked pieces of fish. Beside the charred wood was one boar carcass still waiting to be skinned and a spear stuck in the ground with three strange looking fish impaled on it. Ten feet away from the fire were three leather covered water canteens and a handful of crude but sharp hunting tools, along with a handmade hammock resting above the ground and covered over by a large mosquito net.

They slowly walked down towards the smoldering fire-pit while the only sounds to be heard were the occasional cry of a macaw in the distance and the gurgling slow moving waters of the famous river nearby. The camp appeared to have been swiftly abandoned...until they reached it.

Laughter greeted their ears and they turned to see that an old man was standing against the side of a tree near the hammock, his bare chest and torn jeans covered in dirt and strange camouflage paint. Against the tree in the shadows, the man was almost completely invisible. Only his long white hair and whites of his eyes were barely visible.

He laughed some more and stepped towards them causing Amber and Travis to instinctively back up. Maddox instead just grinned and held his ground saying nothing. Now in the sunlight the old man appeared to be in his eighties, had an emaciated skinny chest, a small goatee, and eyebrows that were so bushy they hid the tops of his eyes. He grabbed a cloth that had been lying beside the bloody boar carcass, and quickly wiped the mud and paint off his face, revealing the happy expression of a man who looked as if he had just won the lottery.

He stepped towards Maddox and took off the famous adventurer's copper tinted sunglasses and examined them closely. He then reached up and touched Maddox's wild spiked hair, puzzled at how it stood straight up. He then looked at the scars around Maddox's eye-sockets from a shark bite months before. He then handed the sunglasses back and spoke with an exotic accent, "You're him, aren't you! The real Maddox Tarver!"

He then waved at Travis and Amber to come closer saying excitedly, "Do you two know who he is!?"

Amber smiled politely, "We've known Maddox for a few years."

"How superb!"

He asked them all to sit and then anxiously gave them each a slice of fish from the pan to eat. Amber hesitated, Maddox thanked the old man, while Travis ate the whole piece in one bite.

"I was fearful you didn't see my smoke signal!"

Maddox bit into the fish on his plate then answered, "I saw soon after we got off the plane. It just took a lot longer to reach you than I wanted."

The jungle man then saw Amber looking back up towards the top of the hill and he said, "Those hooligans will never find us here! I've been watching from the trees and they're still a mile away from here...headed in the wrong direction!"

He then slapped his knee and laughed some more while repeating out loud, "*The wrong direction!*"

Travis and Amber looked at one another a little uneasily, not completely certain of the man's sanity. Maddox instead handed the odd looking key over to him asking, "I found the key the Rogue left you."

The aged jungle explorer looked at the key slowly as he held it up into the sunlight, his eyes suddenly lost in thought as he reflected back to events decades earlier. His expression changed as he turned back to the present and smiled at Maddox and the others.

"I was wondering how long it would take you to discover that the *Rainforest Rogue* and Bounty Hunter fought here in the Amazon!"

Maddox grinned triumphantly, "We found the Bounty Hunter's hideout in the Congo. The clues were all there."

"I suppose before you can use the key you need to know how I saved him."

Amber and Travis looked up in shock.

Travis almost choked on his second helping of cooked fish and looked up incredulously. "You saved the *Rainforest Rogue*???"

The old man handed the key back to Maddox and began with a bombshell statement.

"It wasn't a jail the Bounty Hunter placed the Rogue in. It was a gate meant to keep something out, to keep something from getting into the river."

For the first time since landing in the jungle Maddox looked surprised. "It's *not* a jail??"

"No. A couple years before the Bounty Hunter arrived some European explorers discovered that there were underwater caves and tunnels in this area of the jungle that bordered the Amazon River. They decided they had to investigate further. Big mistake! They quickly found out that some man eater fish or creature lived in the tunnels, and four men were eaten, the fish gobbled them up whole! The survivors quickly escaped and placed five iron bars across the opening which led into the tunnels to keep the horrid creature from swimming out during the flood season."

Amber asked, "I don't understand. Many Bull Sharks and other underwater predators would be able to easily squeeze past any bars."

The old man just shook his head. "This man eater was much, much, much bigger than any Bull Shark! The explorers even built a stone wall inside the tunnel just behind the bars as added protection."

"Oh."

He then continued, "Did those ruffians tell you three about the helmet?"

Maddox nodded his head, "The famous dive helmet covered in gold and jewels."

"Quite right, but did they tell you why they want the helmet?"

Maddox remained quiet while Travis and Amber looked at each other questionably. "We assumed it was worth a lot of money on the black market."

The old man hooted in laughter again but before answering he instead drank water from a pouch made of animal skins, uncaring that some of the water missed and dribbled down his goatee. Putting the pouch aside he excitedly continued, "The Bounty Hunter thought the same, but the Rogue knew better. It is a dive helmet, but so much more! Before the Rogue escaped the steamboat he took the helmet from the boat's safe before swimming for the jungle. He had every right to, the helmet belonged to him! But as you must guess he was recaptured in the jungle. At this point the Bounty Hunter was angrier than a man should ever become, and he trapped the Rogue and shot a harpoon, yes a *harpoon*, right through the Rogue's right leg! But the Rogue had hidden the helmet in the jungle! In punishment the Bounty Hunter had the bars of the gate remade into a sort of prison cell that could swing open, complete with a hand sized padlock to lock it. He then tossed the Rogue in until he would tell him where he hid the treasure."

He then pointed at the rusted key around Maddox's neck and smiled. "Only one key was made, and the Bounty Hunter left it taped inside his slouch hat. He was determined to keep the Rogue in the "jail" for as long as it took. But one man ruined everything for him."

He paused for effect then laughed out loud, "Me! I had been watching everything from the trees the moment that old steamboat appeared down the river. I did not know who this

Rogue was, but I did know the Bounty Hunter by reputation. A nasty man! So one night as a dark storm blotted out the moon and stars I seized the opportunity and snuck on board stealing the key from his cabin! I then swam ashore as the storm got worse and opened the gate to hand the Rogue bandages and some food. He was very thankful...but he refused to leave."

The Rebels continued to listen in quiet amazement as he continued.

"I was afraid his head was damaged mush to say a crazy thing like that! He then told me where the helmet was in the jungle and to bring it to him! Crazy! Crazy! I did as he asked, found the helmet, and gave it to him, all in the dark never once seen by any of the Bounty Hunter's men! Then...boom! The wave hit! The storm was so fierce that the steamboat was spun towards the jungle where it tipped and crashed right onto the shore!! I jumped clear moments before it happened but the Rogue laughed at me and closed the gate...closed it! Saying he would be fine! I barely dove for safety as the boat crashed down right on top of the gate!"

He then pointed to a jagged scar across the width of his entire back, "Cut my back jumping to safety!"

He then paused for a second as the memories continued to return to him.

"The next morning the Bounty Hunter's crew was crazy with anger! Some of his men had died when the boat was toppled, they couldn't right the steamboat, and they had no way now of finding the treasured helmet! But the Bounty Hunter wasn't that angry...because he was happy the Rogue must be dead, trapped underneath the steamboat! Sick man! A week later a cargo plane arrived, piloted by a strange looking fellow who had a thick German accent."

"Wolfgang the Nazi!" Amber exclaimed.

"Who?"

"It doesn't matter, please continue!"

"Now the entire boat's crew hopped on board that plane, and I watched it disappear into the blue sky. I never saw any of those men again! I even heard the Bounty Hunter laugh that no further proof was needed...this Rogue was dead! But I'm a curious man and I wanted proof! So I contacted a tribe of natives I was on good terms with. They agreed to help me and together we went back to the crashed steamboat. Fifty strong men lifted the edge of the boat's hull, just enough for me to look down into the gate."

He then stared at the Rebels his face full of shock.

"It was empty! Empty! It was slowly filling with water, the only sign of the Rogue was that some of the stones inside were covered with his blood...he had vanished! How does a man escape a jail when the only way out is blocked?"

He then took another long drink and concluded his recollection.

"The natives let the steamboat back down, the months passed, then a year, and the steamboat was slowly pushed even further onto the shore by the current, and the beginnings of the swamp began to form around and over it. Then one day the Rogue returned! He simply walked into my camp and handed me the key to the gate! He was limping, but he looked otherwise alright. I asked him how he escaped but he wouldn't answer. He simply told me that one day I or-"

Maddox interrupted asking, "Did he say anything about the helmet?"

"Only that the key would likely be needed to find the treasure, and that he couldn't keep the key anymore. Very strange! He then thanked me and walked back into the jungle. I never saw him again. The years went by, and every single day I tried to figure out the mystery. I wish I could have met him one last time before he died!"

Amber then questioned him, "Do you feel you were ever close to finding the helmet?"

The old jungle explorer waved his hand and exclaimed, "I was never much interested in that! The real mystery to me isn't where he put that helmet, it's how he escaped certain death in that jail buried under the boat! That's the real mystery!"

A quiet moment followed as the Treasure Rebels reflected on the incredible story. With no new questions to ask about the Rogue's escape, Travis brought the conversation back to the present.

"Have you ever heard of a Hector Bragard? He's the one chasing us."

"He's been in the jungle for over a year. I've been able to avoid ever been spotted, watching his men work from the treetops. They have been drilling and searching in every puddle and swamp for a hundred miles. Finally a few weeks ago they arrived here and that...freak of a man ordered his men to cut the steamboat to pieces to find the helmet. I am no expert in the world of treasure recovery, but he looks like a..."

"Vulture." Maddox said.

"Sorry, a what lad?"

Maddox explained, "We call men who are willin' to kill for treasure Vultures."

The jungle man nodded his head in agreement, "That would describe hairy Hector! Then you have experience dealing with criminals like him?"

"We've met more than a few Vultures around the world."

Amber leaned forward intently and asked, "If you've been watching his operations for a year, can you tell us why his men are wearing such strange dive suits instead of scuba gear like Travis and I are wearing?"

The aged jungle nomad listened to her question and replied directly, "The eels!! Those mighty things actually killed some of Hector's men when they first started exploring the swamp. I overheard some of his crew say the suits were designed to be (he paused to remember)...electric eel proof!"

She nodded her head and inquired further, "But why apply modern technology to dive suit designs that are over fifty years old? Especially the oxygen cords?"

The elderly nomad frowned, irritated that he couldn't completely answer her question. He shook his head and said, "I don't know, strangest suits I've ever seen! But I do know those aren't oxygen cords! They supply power to each diver for the drills and other tools they carry! Each cord leads deep into the jungle where Hector and his men are camped!"

He then slowly stood, the carefree grin on his face bigger than ever.

"I have a way for you three to escape Hector the Vulture!"

They followed behind him into the jungle brush, suddenly cutting sharply towards the right. In moments they stood on the bank of the Amazon River where the old man had begun tossing piles of underbrush and leaves into the water...to reveal the sleek outline of a ten year old powerboat painted silver with a few black lines. The Treasure Rebels slowly approached slightly stunned.

Except for a bullet hole in the windscreen and lacking a working radio, the rest of the twenty foot sleek craft was in perfect condition. There were even two plush seats in front of the dashboard, a full tank of gas, and a large throttle that hinted at the boat's immense power. But the most eye catching feature was the boat's peculiarly shaped hull.

The old man didn't waste time explaining how he happened to possess a boat that would have been worth over a hundred thousand dollars when brand new. Instead he simply pointed to the boat's strange shaped hull bobbing above the waterline, "Unique design! Very very rare! Push the yellow button to shut engine down and retract propeller, that works best with the hull. The Rogue would have approved I think!"

He then stepped into the boat without explaining his strange directions and approached the two seats. But he immediately froze and put his hand up for the others to stop, almost shrieking, "Give me the machete!"

Travis and Amber looked at each other again still uneasy of their elderly helper, but Maddox didn't hesitate to hand over the steel blade. Gripping the weapon the old man walked up to the dashboard and the others finally saw what he was looking at.

Crawling atop the wheel was a large spider, almost hairless and completely black, with an arm span of at least 10 inches. It moved slowly, so slowly it gave the appearance of being bored and completely harmless...except for its shiny inch long fangs which reflected off the wheel's chrome. Suddenly it stopped moving as the shadow of the machete covered it.

The elderly jungle man gradually approached, and slowly placed the blade near the arachnid until the creature climbed onto it. Then with a yell he snapped his wrist toward the boat's edge, tossing the spider far over the side, where it flipped end over end a couple times before dropping into the slow moving river with a faint *plopping* sound, never to resurface. The old man turned, his sun beaten wrinkled skin suddenly white.

"Of all my years in this jungle, that is by far the biggest arachnid I have ever seen. Ever!! I would reckon it is the largest spider in any jungle in the world!!"

Travis remembered back to the spiders in the Congo and trying to keep a straight face replied, "Uh yeah...probably."

All four then spent the next few minutes searching the powerboat for any snakes, spiders, or scorpions. They didn't find any, but they did find the broken remains of another old diving helmet, similar to the one covered in mildew in the cave. Except this dive helmet was completely shattered into multiple pieces.

He then showed them exactly how the powerboat operated, then finished by pointing upriver while he explained, "Follow the river that way until you meet the Brazilian police by the coast. Come another day to find the treasure helmet! Hector and his men will never see you leave the jungle in time, and without the Rogue's key they will never find the treasure either!"

He then handed the machete back to Maddox and stepped off the boat onto the grass. He then turned and faced the spikey haired adventurer.

"The world's gotten so bad since my glory days, I've tended to think all the heroes are in the past." He then pointed at Maddox, "Seeing you...I realize I've been thinking wrong."

Maddox was too stunned to say much but the simple words, "Thanks, man."

By the dashboard Amber noticed the old jungle explorer had jumped ashore and called out, "You should come with us! It's only a matter of time until Hector finds your campsite!"

"No need to worry young lady. The whole jungle is my campsite!"

He then waved goodbye to Travis and Amber before vanishing from their sight into the shadows of the rainforest.

"What a weird yet likable old man."

Travis replied, "If he saved the *Rogue* that makes him more cool than weird."

Maddox wasn't listening to either of them, instead he was looking towards the jungle lost in thought, his eyes slightly watery behind the sunglasses as he reflected with humble pride on what the old man had said.

The moment passed, and he quickly handed the machete to Travis before stepping up to the driver's wheel. With a big smile he grabbed the ignition key and turned it to the right, bringing the powerboat's engine screaming to life.

The Treasure Rebels were headed down the Amazon River.

==================

Hector Bragard slowly drank the last of his brandy then swished the drink around in his mouth before spitting the alcohol and the remains of a broken tooth onto the ground. He grinned wolfishly and said, "Who needs a dentist!"

When none of his crew laughed the smile quickly morphed into a sneer, and the behemoth of a man threw the canteen against a tree in rage, the aluminum shell cracking in two as it smashed into the trunk. With all of his hired men watching he slowly stepped out of the shadows and into the boiling sun.

Hector Bragard looked like a long lost descendent of Blackbeard...only more disturbing looking. He was a monstrous six foot nine in height and had a long black beard which hung down below his neck, every strand twisted and dirty looking. Pushing fifty, the front half of his head was completely bald, and he had unwisely decided to let the back half of his hair grow to such a length it hung down between his shoulder blades to his lower back. His hands were twice the size of a normal man's, and his entire body was hardened and chiselled from years living in brutal extreme climates. Both of his ears had missing pieces, thanks to frostbite from an Arctic expedition a year before. His nose was also punctured in five different places with gold nose rings which glittered in the sun. He wore military style pants and a black shirt with no sleeves, exposing arms covered in odd tattoos.

At first glance he looked like a professional bodybuilder similar to Ted Claymire, only bigger and nastier looking. But in reality Hector was not just Ted's superior in strength, but also in artefact thefts. Over the last decade he had become of the wealthiest black market thieves on the planet, and he used his immoral wealth to hire a team of scuba divers and former soldiers who shared his love of money and dislike for even the most basic of ethics.

Hector and his men were standing atop a fifty-foot hill a half mile from the swamp, the rainforest spread out in every direction below them. At this location and height the Amazon River was mostly obscured by the jungle tree tops, but they were still close enough to hear the river water as it flowed through the rainforest below.

He turned to his eight men who were of various nationalities. "See them?" Two of the men pulled binoculars away from their eyes and shook their heads in frustration.

"Nothing Mr. Bragard."

He then turned to Ted and Sharen who sat on the jungle grass with their arms handcuffed.

"Who are these three again?"

Ted grimaced as he shifted his weight, his right hand still burning with pain from the broken fingers and wrist caused when he had punched Bragard back at the swamp. Bragard hadn't blinked when Ted's knuckles cracked into the side of his mouth cutting the tooth in two. Ted instead felt as if the inside of his hand had detonated into a million pieces at the impact.

"I said already, the Treasure Rebels."

Bragard grunted in irritation and replied, "The Treasure Rebels are media darlings. Little celebrities the press made famous without merit."

While no fan of the Rebels himself, Ted still wanted to point out to his hairy captor that Maddox and his friends had discovered millions of dollars of hidden treasure, and that the media hadn't been able to keep up with reporting all of their discoveries. But he wisely chose to keep quiet.

Despite his derisive comments Bragard also knew the Treasure Rebels were the best treasure hunters in the world. It was their ability to escape him, and his jealousy of their achievements, that stirred up his dangerous temper.

"Are they carrying guns?"

"Underwater?"

Hector turned to Sharen.

"What's the range of their radio?"

She scowled back, "If it was turned on you'd be able to track the signal. They must have disabled it right after you threatened them."

Irritated he walked over to the hill's edge and turned to look down at the expansive jungle. His teeth were grating with anger as he struggled to decide what to do next. Suddenly in the distance the faint dim rattle of an engine echoed from beneath the trees. He listened carefully and the angry scowl across his face was replaced with an arrogant smirk.

"I hear a motorboat along the river. Get the *Scimitar*."

==================

As he spoke the Treasure Rebels two miles away skimmed across the river's surface, their powerboat's long wake concealed by the thick tree branches hanging overhead.

"I remember from reading old journals and diaries that there are myths that some of the early explorers, even pirates, were attacked by some sort of jungle monster. I'm willing to believe they might have seen something, but the stories are too preposterous to take as fact. Especially considering the sightings were said to have been first reported by a known pirate of the time."

Travis shook his head and disagreed with Amber.

"After the crazy things we've seen the last couple months I think the ol' pirate could have been telling the truth."

They continued in silence for another ten minutes as they watched the shoreline for any animal or sign of their pursuers.

Amber finally turned her attention back to the others and asked, "What do you think this nutty Hector will do to the Claymires after we escape?"

Travis shrugged his shoulders, "Ted and Sharen will have to convince him they know where the helmet is or they're toast."

"The Claymires are creeps, but I hate to leave them behind as Bragard's prisoners."

Maddox pushed the throttle to the next level and as the boat increased speed he replied, "Ted and Sharen may have already struck a deal to work with a corrupt dude like Hector. They don't look like the kind who would put up much of a fight when pressured."

Amber rested her arm on the side of the boat and looked at Maddox puzzled. "This isn't like you Maddox, so eager to get away from the action."

"Whatever has happened, us getting to the cops is the best option to save or arrest the Claymires, and to have Hector and his Vultures stopped as well."

Suddenly a perceptive look crossed Amber's face.

"And the sooner we can then search the swamp for the helmet."

Maddox's usual grin returned. "Exactly."

He then turned the wheel to the left and the powerboat smoothly cut through a long curve in the river. But just as the water pathway straightened out he had to pull back on the throttle...as a large river boat almost the entire width of the river was blocking their path, anchored horizontally so as to block all boats from continuing past. It had two decks, was painted light blue, and the name *Bloody Scimitar VI* was visible in white paint on the side.

Maddox instinctively spun the wheel as Amber and Travis held on...only to see two speedboats sporting mounted machine guns approaching them only three hundred yards from the other direction.

They were trapped.

Maddox spun the wheel again to face the river boat, except now they could see that four gunmen, Hector, and the still handcuffed Claymires were standing by the top rail overlooking the water.

Hector looked down at the Treasure Rebels, his wild beard and strange mullet blowing in the jungle wind. He gripped the rail so tightly the metal rung actually groaned as the steel was twisted under his grip.

The speedboats glided to a slow crawl a hundred yards away and waited for further orders, while Hector yelled over the dull rhythm of the faint engine noises. He didn't mince words.

"Do you have my helmet?"

Maddox yelled back, "What makes you certain we have it?"

Hector's grotesque mouth twisted into an even more grotesque smile.

"If you don't, then I kill your employers!"

He then nodded at his men who lifted their handguns in display and pointed them at Ted and Sharen.

Travis grunted quietly, "He thinks we were workin' for them! I wonder how many lies they told that hairy monster to stay alive."

Maddox was barely listening to his friend, instead he studied the two riverbank sides on each end of the river boat. He called up to his bearded enemy, "We're willing to surrender the helmet! But we want you to release our...employers first!"

Hector scratched at the nose rings as he thought over Maddox's offer.

"*NO!*"

Amber noticed Maddox's gaze towards the riverbanks and guessed at what he was thinking. "Maddox even with the flooding there must only be four feet between the river boat and the shore...not enough to squeeze past."

Maddox didn't respond to her, instead he yelled and pointed at the mud covered grass lining the river.

"Just put them on the river bank man! Then we'll hand it over directly to you!"

He then lifted one of the pieces of the broken dive helmet that belonged to the old jungle man, just enough for the sunlight to reflect off of it before he lowered it hurriedly back into the boat. From this distance it was impossible for Hector to tell if the helmet was authentic, or to see that the helmet was no longer in one piece. To Maddox's relief no one else standing by the rail had been using a pair of binoculars either.

Hector wrongly mistook the sunlight's reflection off the old metal helmet for gold. His greed filled hunger took centre stage in his thoughts and he was now certain that Maddox did indeed have the mysterious treasure he had wanted for years. But he still wouldn't budge.

"No! My men will pull up alongside your boat. Once they have my helmet I will let the Claymires go ashore."

Maddox called back to Travis, "Grab the chainsaw."

He then handed the helmet fragment to a puzzled Amber as Travis pulled the underwater chainsaw out of the sheath behind his back.

Maddox then called back up to Hector, "Wrong move man! Our way, or else we cut the helmet to pieces!"

Understanding what Maddox now meant, Travis lifted the chainsaw for everyone to see on the river boat, then dramatically he pushed the red trigger and the chain came to life cutting through the air with an intense metallic shriek. When Hector only responded by stunned silence, Amber turned her back to the riverboat and made a show of holding the helmet in front of Travis who brought the chainsaw done towards it.

"ENOUGH! I AGREE*!"

His bald forehead suddenly dripping with anxious sweat he ordered his men to take the Claymires to the deck below and then put them ashore. On the powerboat Travis turned the chainsaw off and placed it back into the sheath while Amber put the helmet piece back under her seat still hidden from view.

"Maddox, we can't fit past the river boat. Four feet isn't enough."

"You forgot this powerboat only needs four feet."

"What?"

They watched as two of Hector's men obeyed his orders and forced the Claymires at gunpoint down the steps onto the main deck. Ted and Sharen then happily jumped across the four foot gap to shore, only to realize that the two gunmen followed behind them to wait until Maddox had handed the helmet over to their boss.

"Amber take the wheel."

"Maddox! Where am I steering?"

"Right for the Claymires."

She continued to protest then stopped as she remembered the shape of the powerboat's hull and the mysterious instructions from the old jungle man.

A small grin crossed her face.

"How fast do you think it needs?"

"As much as possible without throwing us overboard."

He then stood up and waved at Hector who now stood at the lower rail on the main deck. "We give you the helmet now!"

Hector' ugly smile grew larger...and uglier.

"Agreed! I'm waiting!"

Maddox then left the dashboard to stand beside Travis. Slowly Amber pushed the throttle forward and they began to move towards the *Scimitar*. Behind them Hector's two speedboats slowly followed.

Travis now understood as well and asked, "What about our *employers*? Are we leaving them behind?"

"Nice if we could!"

"Maddox! Of course not!" Amber called back at him.

They pretended not to have heard her then took positions on the right side of the powerboat, securing their feet so they wouldn't tumble over the side.

She turned back to the wheel and increased the throttle a little more. They moved to within a hundred feet of Hector' river boat. Then ninety. Then eighty. The seconds passed and soon they were only fifty feet from the *Scimitar*.

Full throttle.

The powerboat blasted forward, leaving a wild spray of water fifty feet into the sky behind them. She turned the wheel to the right, heading directly for the shore where Ted and

Sharen stood still as if they were deer frozen by a car's headlights.

The two mercenaries guarding them opened fire but their aim was off and they quickly jumped towards the safety of the jungle. Hector's men on the *Scimitar* were caught off guard as well and by the time they started shooting the Treasure Rebels were almost out of their line of sight.

Just before they hit the small gap between the *Scimitar* and land, Amber hit the yellow switch. Power to the engine was instantly cut while the propeller stopped and was pulled up into a special compartment under the hull.

The powerboat still continued tearing across the water at an incredible speed due to the forward momentum, and just before the powerboat hit the grass Amber turned sharply to the left. The powerboat rocketed into the four foot gap between the *Scimitar* and shore with one side in the water while the other skimmed across the wet grass thanks to the specialized hull design. Maddox and Travis reached out and grabbed Ted and Sharen right off their feet, pulling them directly into the powerboat as they rocketed past.

The two thieves hit the deck roughly but didn't care. They were alive, and the very people they had captured a week earlier had just rescued them from their own criminal captors.

The powerboat tore through the rest of the gap and Amber quickly turned the wheel back while pressing the yellow switch again. The propeller lowered back into the water and began spinning furiously again as the engine came back to life.

They were in the clear.

Amber pushed the throttle to FULL POWER then took a split second to look back.

"Everyone okay?"

Travis and Maddox both gave the thumbs up sign while Ted and Sharen were still too stunned to do anything other than quickly nod their heads to signal yes. Amber turned back to the dials in front of her while the sound of gunfire and Hector shrieking in uncontrolled fury could be heard far behind them.

"Goodbye Hector" she muttered under her breath.

Behind them one of the speedboats tried to give chase by trying to ride the top of the river's edge the same way Amber had done. It didn't work.

Without the special hull design the enemy speedboat smashed into the shore with a loud screech and Bragard's hired Vulture at the wheel lost complete control. The twin propellers were both shredded off, and one actually embedded into the side of the *Scimitar's* painted wooden hull. The speedboat then became airborne and began flipping end over end towards the jungle trees, tossing both men on board clear into the rainforest. The boat finally came down, smashing off the base of two tree trunks until it exploded into an orange red fire ball. Both Vultures stumbled back towards the *Scimitar*, one with a separated shoulder and lacerated arm, the other with a now deformed broken nose covered in red blood that no surgery would ever be able to fix properly.

Within minutes the Treasure Rebels were already two miles ahead and Amber easily steered through the winding path just as the river itself began to widen and the jungle brush hanging over the water began to thin out. Suddenly she called back to the others and pointed up to their right.

"The plane!"

Everyone looked up and sure enough they could faintly see the Phenom 300 high above the trees resting on the hillside. Suddenly an idea hit Maddox and he turned to Ted who still sat on the deck catching his breath.

"Did Hector leave any of his men with the plane?"

Ted responded between gasps for breath, "No...he killed our last man...so he figured there was no one around to take it back...He wanted everyone to search for you three."

Maddox quickly nodded to Travis and they both left the Claymires to talk with Amber at the dashboard.

"Maddox has an idea."

Amber didn't take her eyes off the river, "I'm listening guys."

Maddox pointed up at the small jet plane. "A lot of our dive equipment is still stored on the Phenom."

Amber's expression slowly became more apprehensive. "Okay..."

"And if we leave the plane Bragard will use it to easily escape before the boys in blue arrive. It'll take us at least three more hours to reach any help, and probably another hour for the government to assemble a team large enough to arrest them. He'll be long gone...and that hairy Vulture will then follow us all over the world thinkin' we got his helmet."

"I understand Maddox but Hector must have his own aircraft. He probably wouldn't risk using the Claymire's no matter how close it is. He'll just trek another couple hours through the jungle to wherever he hid his own plane."

"That makes it even more urgent to use the radio in the plane before he flies away...plus you'll get your tablet back."

She paused for a moment then replied, "Okay guys I agree. But I hate to leave the boat when all we have to do is sit back and ride out of this place."

Travis grinned, "Think of it this way, we'll be in the sky and out of the rainforest ten times sooner than if we stay with the river."

"I like that. But what about the Claymires? Do you think we can trust them enough to come along?"

They looked back and saw Ted and Sharen studying the broken pieces of the dive helmet they had used to trick Hector, a look of satisfaction on their faces. Ted looked up at them and yelled smugly, "So the 'Treasure Rebels couldn't find the treasure either!"

The Rebels looked back at each other, all thinking and saying the same thing: "No!" The Claymires could never be trusted.

Travis then scratched his head and wondered out loud, "They won't agree. How do we keep em' on the boat?"

They paused for a second until Maddox eyed the handcuffs on Ted's hands. "Still have the lock-picks?" Travis patted one of the hidden waterproof pockets on his diving suit. "Yep."

Amber steered the powerboat to a stop next to the shore, then Claymire brother and sister were ordered to get up and stand next to the dashboard. Travis then used the lock pick to unfasten then re-lock their handcuffs to the wheel. Meanwhile Amber explained that if they continued to follow the river they would escape before Hector could catch them. Ted and Sharen remained silent, uncertain as to what the Rebels were planning. Once Maddox and his team jumped off the boat onto the grass to head into the jungle, they realized with fury they were going for their plane.

"Tarver!!"

Maddox turned as the Bounty Hunter's grandson made one last nasty statement.

"A fame seeking treasure hunter little punk like you is nothing! You will never compare to my grandfather! And you will *never* find the helmet!"

Against Travis and Amber's protest Maddox walked back to the boat to stand in front of his defeated enemy. He looked up at Ted from the shore, the waters of the Amazon reflecting off his sunglasses.

"Your right man, I am nothing like the Bounty Hunter...and that's why I 'm going to succeed where your sick granddaddy failed."

He then re-joined his friends and together they disappeared into the Amazon jungle and began their run up the hillside towards the plane. By the water Ted continued screaming towards the trees but his shrieks were never answered. The Rebels were gone. He then dejectedly pushed the throttle forward and together with Sharen they piloted the boat up the Amazon River, apprehensively looking back every few seconds to see if Hector and his men were following.

The minutes flew past and every step the Rebels drew closer to the Phenom 300. Maddox hacked mercilessly with the machete at every branch and tree limb that blocked their path. Still dressed in their dive suits, Amber and Travis felt as if they were almost suffocating from the jungle heat, and even Maddox's sunglasses were covered and dripping with sweat from his forehead.

After a half hour had passed they finally paused for a five minute break by the side of a small bubbling ravine which twisted across their path before disappearing through the trees and down the side of the hill. Maddox knelt beside the ravine and carelessly threw handful after handful of water into his face. In moments Travis and Amber followed, but no one drank the water for fear of getting an intestinal parasite.

A minute passed and then with a nod from Maddox they all stood and began climbing again. The hill became steeper and the jungle pathway more crowded with hanging tree limbs, exotic colourful plants, and the occasional boar or small deer that leaped out of their way in a hurried panic.

Twenty minutes later the intense climb came to an end, and they finally stepped past the jungle growth and onto the open clearing at the top of the hill. The Phenom 300 sat quietly in the sunlight two hundred feet away. They waited and listened before moving towards the plane. Only stillness greeted their ears and they could see that behind the cockpit glass the pilot's chairs were still empty.

They then quickly ran across the thick grass to the open air-stairs. Amber was the first one to climb up, followed by Travis. Maddox paused at the base of the air-stairs and studied the jungle plateau far below the hill. Still no sign of their enemy.

He quickly ascended the steps four at a time.

Inside the aircraft they were greeted with fierce humidity as the jungle heat had gotten into the plane's main cabin long ago. They immediately closed the air-stairs and Amber hit the ON button for the A/C. In two seconds cool refreshing air began pumping through the vents near the leather seats, and the air temperature began to drop.

They quickly searched the plane's main cabin and equipment room at the back to make sure none of Hector' men had stayed behind. Now certain they were alone, Maddox and Travis went straight for the cockpit.

Amber instead began rummaging through every cabinet to find her tablet computer, ignoring the small tables covered with maps and the Claymires' tin replica of the treasure which was stored atop a small fridge. She finally came to the last cabinet which was locked. Pulling out the lock-pick from her own dive suit she began to work the keyhole. In moments the lock clicked and the mahogany door popped open to reveal her one of a kind computer inside. She grabbed it and tapped the screen a half dozen times, then stood and smiled. The tablet's security system had never been breached. She then opened the fridge and grabbed three ice cold bottles of pop.

Entering the cockpit she found Maddox chatting in Portuguese with air control through the radio while Travis was studying a digital map on a large screen. She handed out the drinks and after another minute Maddox ended the call. He took a long drink then explained, "They're sending an armed police team here to the swamp to grab Hector, and they'll have other officers waitin' for Ted and Sharen on the river. They want us to radio back once we're surfin' above the jungle."

He then tossed the empty bottle back into the main cabin behind the cockpit and began the pre-flight procedures while Travis and Amber buckled up.

Showtime.

The multiple jet engines roared to life and Maddox increased the power. The jet plane picked up speed and began rolling across the empty plateau towards the edge overlooking the swamp. There was just enough "runway" and with forty feet to spare Maddox pulled the Phenom 300 clear of the jungle grass and into the blue sky.

They were greeted with an incredible view of the Amazon Rainforest and the mysterious swamp below them...and then suddenly the flash of a rocket screaming past the cockpit before tearing directly through the left wing!

The plane immediately dropped like a stone, and despite Maddox's best efforts he couldn't stabilize the aircraft. A large fireball crackled and spit flame where most of the wing had been, and the muddy waters of the mysterious swamp filled the cockpit window view as the plane descended towards the water. In the final few seconds Maddox managed to straighten the plane and slow down the rapid descent, causing the aircraft to skip across the swamp's surface instead of crashing straight into it.

The plane shrieked and groaned at the violent impact as the hull was bent in multiple places. The end of the tail splintered into two warped parts, and the fireball hissed and turned into a rising cloud of steam as the flames were engulfed by the swamp water. The aircraft tilted to one side, what remained of the destroyed wing dipping beneath the surface. The entire aircraft then began to slowly sink into the dark water.

Inside the cockpit Maddox and the others slowly unbuckled and climbed out of their seats, stunned and livid with anger. They looked through the cracked cockpit window and hated what they saw.

Slowly approaching the plane were three speedboats, each one containing men armed with weapons. Standing in the last speedboat was Hector, grinning malevolently, the rocket launcher he had used still discharging smoke and sitting on his shoulder.

Amber turned to her friends.

"You guys all right?"

Travis wiped the thin cut across his head then spat some of the blood that had trickled down into his mouth, "Hector won't be once I get out of here."

"Maddox?"

Maddox didn't respond, instead he kept looking at Hector in the distance as the professional criminal drew closer.

"Maddox?"

He still didn't answer but instead whirled and dove at Amber and Travis, pushing them both backward and into the main cabin just before bullets began to spray the cockpit. They climbed back to their feet and Maddox slammed the cockpit door closed.

"He thinks the helmet is on the plane. He's just gonna kill us then search for it."

They then looked out through the small windows of the main cabin and could see that the three speedboats had split up and were now approaching the destroyed plane from different directions. They were surrounded.

Travis spat again in rage, "Ted and Sharen must have left a few guns on board! We can hold them off."

Amber looked out the window once again and saw that the waterline had risen even closer to the glass.

"But Travis then what? Even if they don't get inside the whole plane will sink in minutes! There's nowhere for us to go but down!"

Maddox's expression abruptly changed as his anger completely vanished.

"Gnarly idea!"

PART IV: OPENING THE "PRISON" GATE

Hector and his men quietly slowed their three speedboats to a stop after circling the sinking plane for five minutes. They had stopped shooting long ago and Hector impatiently waited for a hatch to open. His eyes never seemed to blink and when a leech crawled out of his beard and began to suck blood out of the side of his nose he barely noticed. He finally ripped the slimy creature free and tossed it into the water, his extreme dark eyes never leaving the aircraft.

"Let's just blast our way in."

Hector lifted his tattooed hand in disagreement. "No. I don't want my helmet being destroyed. The little rats will step out when they have to choose between facing us or drowning."

The mercenary disagreed, "But what if they just dump the helmet into the swamp?"

Hector wiped the blood trickling down the side of his nose courtesy of the leech. He then pointed at the wooden pier where a dozen of his team's high tech dive suits had been left behind. "Then we shoot them, put on our dive gear, pull up the helmet before nightfall, and leave this unpleasant jungle rich men." He then turned back to the plane just in time to see the air-stairs hatch open with a soft hiss.

Suddenly the plane began to descend into the swamp at a faster pace and the fuselage began to slowly spin upwards, causing the open hatch to now face the sky above. The Treasure Rebels climbed out and stood atop the fuselage and looked down at Hector and his men as the plane continued to sink.

Maddox now wore one of their own customized scuba suits, while Travis and Amber sported new dive masks and air tanks all from the equipment room inside the plane.

Travis also carried the Claymire's tin replica of the treasured dive helmet, pretending to strain as if it weighed over fifty pounds. The sun lit up the painted replica brilliantly and the reflection gave the surface of the water around the plane a gold tint. Maddox pointed at the helmet then signalled Hector to draw closer.

Hector smirked victoriously and steered the boat slowly forward. He whispered into a hand held radio to all his men. "Do not shoot. Lower your firearms. Wait till the little scuba rats hand it over. The man who shoots loses his cut of the profits. Understood?"

The radio crackled in response as every man surrounding the sinking plane mumbled "Yes sir."

The mercenary beside Hector replied angrily, "Look at their dive equipment! Are we just going to let them swim away!"

Hector didn't bother to reply, instead he spoke again into the handheld radio. "Blow the charges we placed by the cave they escaped in before."

In one of the other boats another mercenary pushed a small switch and a dull roar rumbled from below the water.

Hector turned back to the man questioning him.

"With the cave sealed off they have nowhere to escape."

His ugly bearded face twisted into a triumphant yet warped smile and he patted the rifle slung over his thickset shoulder blade. "Let em' swim down there all day! When they run out of oxygen and resurface they'll have to face this!"

The speedboats pulled as close as possible to the descending plane without risking being sucked into the water was well, and Hector looked up at his seemingly beaten opponents.

"*Give me my helmet*!"

Travis lifted the replica in Hector's direction and nodded his head towards Maddox and Amber.

He understood and shouted, "I agree."

Maddox and Amber both jumped clear of the plane and disappeared below the surface as all of the mercenaries ignored them. All eyes were instead focused on Travis and the "gold" helmet.

Travis then lifted the replica as if preparing to toss it...then suddenly dropped it straight back into the plane through the open hatch! Hector shrieked in fury and before anyone could react Travis had jumped backwards into the dark water...and was gone.

Ten seconds later the entire criminal gang watched in agony as the brownish water poured into the open hatchway as the plane finally went completely under. Then their disbelief and anger only intensified as one of the giant electric eels curled out of the water right where the plane had been moments before...then twisting downward it snaked into the plane through the now submerged hatch as the plane continued to sink towards the swamp's muddy bottom.

Hector finally snapped out of his paralyzed shock and shrieked at his men while pointing at their unusual dive suits sitting on the rotting pier. "*NOW*!!" Every mercenary dreaded the thought of entering the plane with the eel still inside, but they instantly followed his order and raced across the swamp towards the suits.

Far below the churning speedboats the Treasure Rebels quickly swam towards the rusted remains of the steamboat. No eel or other creature crossed their path.

They didn't speak a word, not wasting a single second or breath. The steamboat finally materialized and they swam hurriedly inside the opening in the rusted hull, following Maddox as they had before through the twisted steel beams and warped rotted timber of the steamboats' central staircase. They finally reached the opening which led into the cave, but as they had feared it had been destroyed by explosives, the opening now completely obstructed with dirt, stones, and a few pieces of charred bent steel.

Travis instinctively lifted the chainsaw out of its holster.

Maddox raised his arm. "No it'll take too long man."

"We got time! Lets' try using the saws to bore a hole for us to swim through."

Maddox instead pointed towards the shadowy interior of the steamboat's ruined insides.

"Let's escape the way the *Rainforest Rogue* did instead."

Travis re-sheathed the chainsaw and looked at Amber who also stared back speechless. They both then began to ask Maddox what he meant but he was already moving into the shadows. Puzzled but hopeful they followed.

Under normal conditions they never would have swum through the insides of any kind of underwater boat or wreck without specialized equipment and a team of people to assist them. Many professional divers had died while becoming trapped or confused while searching the insides of a wreck.

Only a fool would swim inside without taking the proper safety precautions, and the Treasure Rebels were no fools. But with Hector about to kill them they had no choice but to swim through for a way out.

Maddox suddenly stopped kicking and hovered over a stretch of the steel hull where two large steel beams had pierced through the metal from outside.

"This is it, the gate is right between the two beams."

"Maddox how do you know that?"

He didn't explain but had already begun cutting into the steel with his chainsaw. Certain they'd get a complete answer later Amber and Travis then lifted their own chainsaws out and together all three of the Treasure Rebels began carefully slicing into the corroded hull.

=================

At that very moment six of Hector's men carefully approached the sunken Phenom 300. If asked the underwater criminals couldn't have explained how they felt. They believed that sitting in the plane was a treasure worth more than fifty million dollars...and an electric eel that had already killed some of their friends. They trusted Hector and were confident that the suits would withstand whatever voltage the creature was capable of discharging. They not only trusted him, but shared his obsession with greed. But unlike Hector they weren't insane. So despite his shouting into their earpieces that they were to hurry, they took their time and carefully approached the dark hatchway.

As the plane had descended the fuselage had spun a little to the left, and the hatchway was now only five feet above the swamp mud. One of the men pulled out a glow stick specially designed for underwater use, and when everyone signalled they were ready he tossed it through the hatchway. The interior of the plane lit up and the men looked inside through the circular windows. They gulped in alarm as they saw the giant eel was still inside and curled around one of the posh leather seats...chewing on the helmet!

In a panic they threw every glow stick they possessed into the plane, hoping the bright lights would scare the monster eel out. The plan worked and the massive creature shot out of the plane in fright, its long body snapping back and forth as it rocketed threw the water. The electric creature paid no attention to the six divers standing by the plane, and it didn't even feel its tail smack into the glass faceplate of one of the men. The mercenary stumbled back and collapsed into the mud disoriented as the fifteen foot creature disappeared into the murkiness. While one of the other divers helped the man up, the other four didn't care and were already crawling inside the sunken plane. In a few moments the tin helmet was lifted proudly out of the hatchway, the blue glow stick lights reflecting off the "gold."

The criminals cheered in triumph, unable to tell that the helmet was an imitation and worth little more than forty dollars.

"Wait till Hector sees it!"

"He'll finally calm down!"

==================

Deep within the steamboat's ruins the Treasure Rebels continued to cut through the steel hull. Finally they replaced the chainsaws in their holsters and together lifted the large slice of cut steel free...to reveal below the five iron bars of the "prison" gate and the tarnished silver padlock still attached to it.

Maddox lifted the key off his neck and placed it into the padlock. With a quick snap of his wrist a dull echo sounded through the water as the lock inside turned and the padlock released from the bars and drifted down into the steamboat, unlocked for the first time in over half a century.

The gate opened with a loud screech and they swam inside.

The inside of the "jail" was only about five feet wide and high, with only about six feet of depth. The entire back wall was filled with large stones. Despite the long passage of time the European's handiwork from decades ago remained intact. Travis tested the stones and marvelled at their strength, "So this is what Hector and his buddies were preparing to drill through."

Amber lifted her tablet and swept it across the stone wall, scanning every rock covered inch. She then lifted the screen towards her face and read the findings. "Guys it's only a foot deep in places! It appears to be the weakest at the-"

"Over here."

Maddox pointed to three of the largest stones near the right side. "Travis, hit that one. Amber, that one. I'll smash this stone."

Surprised she replaced her tablet inside her dive suit sleeve and pulled out the chainsaw as Travis and Maddox were doing. They each took their positions and then at the same time they swung the butt end of their chainsaws into a different stone.

All three stones shot forward into the darkness beyond the "jail" wall, and instantly the entire wall crumbled under the weight of the water which now poured through, sucking all three treasure hunters into the cavern beyond.

They slowly stood as their goggle dive lights illuminated an empty cavern of natural black stone which sloped upwards for twenty feet. Behind them water continued to pour inside from the swamp. There was nowhere to go but back into the swamp or walk up the slope into the cavern above them. Amber's tablet beeped twice to signal the air was safe and they disconnected their dive masks from their oxygen tanks. Keeping the masks on they swept the cavern with their goggle lights as they climbed to the top and stepped into the unknown.

The bright lights illuminated an even larger cavern, eight times as big as the one behind the "jail." The enormous space was completely empty except for a fifteen foot pool of water in the very centre.

Amber swept the tablet over the black water and looked at the readings. "It's deep."

They nodded to one another, reattached their masks to the tanks, and jumped in.

=================

High above the underground cavern Hector smashed the replica helmet underneath the heel of his black boot. Pieces of tin flew in every direction as the pier shook at the violent force of his boot striking the wooden plank. He then coldly snapped his fingers and pointed at his own specialized dive suit on shore. In a split second his men were scrambling to bring it to him. Then with a voice so filled with resentment and rage it sounded like an eerie hoarse hiss, he pointed back at the swamp.

"We dive on the steamboat."

==================

The Treasure Rebels realized that they were swimming in a shallow naturally made underground tunnel, and there was nowhere to swim but forward. The water was pitch black, and their three dive mask lights cut through the darkness with the precision of a laser forty feet ahead of them. As they kicked their fins and pushed forward they encountered no fish or any other sign of underwater life, except for the occasional odd looking plant or clump of grass growing out of the tunnels mud walls.

"I don't like this. There should be *some* aquatic life."

Amber suggested, "It might mean were swimming in the hunting area of an alpha predator."

"I know. That's why I don't like it."

Maddox was quiet as he swam slightly ahead of his two friends, the light from his mask therefore reaching further into the tunnel than theirs. Suddenly he stopped kicking and broke his silence.

"Piranha."

Amber and Travis pulled up beside him...to see *hundreds* of piranha appear out of the darkness and swim directly towards them!

They spun and swam back in the opposite direction but it in seconds dozens of the red bellied flesh eaters with their black eyes and glistening white jagged teeth had reached their fins, their legs, and then their heads.

But the piranha never bit into them. Instead the small predators kept swimming forward, and the water around the Rebels became a blur as dozens and dozens of the creatures swam past their field of vision. Maddox correctly guessed what was happening.

"Something's chasing them!"

Instinctively they paused for a split second to look back, their dive lights once again illuminating the tunnel from the direction the piranha were coming from. They weren't prepared for what they saw.

Only five yards from their kicking legs was a monstrous piranha like creature over ten feet long and four feet wide. Its body was covered in silvery coloured scales and it shared a similar dead looking pair of black eyes like the smaller piranha. But unlike the piranha the monster sized fish had very different teeth, sporting two immense fangs each twenty-four inches long at the bottom of its mouth, each white tooth disappearing into a slot in the top of its jaws when its mouth closed. It was a Payara, one of the Amazon's most famous underwater predators. And it was immensely larger in size than any previously recorded.

The Payara reached the school of piranha and began furiously chomping away. Instantly a half dozen piranha were cut in half, serrated by the two hideously long bottom fangs, while a couple simply disappeared into the Payara's huge jaws never to swim out again.

The water was suddenly full of half-chewed and severed piranha. The surviving flesh eaters shot forward faster in the water to escape the same death while Maddox and his friends found an extra gear and swam with everything they had. The monstrous fish instead easily picked up speed and continued eating, drawing even closer to the Rebels' kicking fins.

When they were within twenty feet of reaching the cavern, the school of piranha around them suddenly made a sharp turn upwards and to the right. Amber and Travis ignored them and continued forward. Swimming a couple feet behind Maddox instead turned his head to watch and his dive light revealed the piranha were swimming up into a hidden crevice they hadn't spotted before.

Feeling the two giant fangs of the "vampire" fish barely scrape against his fins, he correctly guessed he wasn't going to make it all the way to the end. So he gambled. Turning suddenly he swam up and the right as well, following the school of piranha up into the crevice. The monster sized creature gave up on him and the smaller piranha and instead zeroed in on Travis and Amber who had just reached the end of the tunnel.

"You go first!"

Before she could argue with Travis he spun in the water and pulled out the chainsaw in one motion. Just as she climbed out back into the cavern he pressed the chainsaw's red button. The chain roared to life and he swung it furiously at the approaching Payara.

But he missed.

The giant predator easily curved away from the serrated chain to Travis' right, spinning in a full circle before cutting down towards him with its jaws wide open. He lifted the chainsaw up in front of his face as a last defence and the two foot long fangs sliced directly into the chainsaw's mechanical guts. The chain instantly stopped spinning and the creature began to shake violently back and forth to free itself of the weapon which had become trapped between its two enormous fangs.

Travis was pushed backwards by the violent force of the creature's bite, but the Payara had only tasted the chainsaw, not him. He looked up and saw Amber's hand reaching down through the water towards him. He grasped it and kicking his legs furiously he broke the water's surface and climbed out to safety.

They had made it.

==================

Maddox continued to follow the surviving piranha who swam through the crevices' winding path upward. The crevice itself was only five feet wide, and Maddox followed slowly to ensure his tank didn't catch on a protruding stone, or worse, that he would get stuck and trapped forever.

The piranha suddenly dispersed ahead of him and he realized that the crevice ended and opened up into another body of water. He swam through and left the oppressive crevice behind to see he was inside another pool of water in the centre of a small cave. Fresh jungle air whistled throughout the cave from a large opening in the far side, where the water from the pool flowed out into a slow moving ravine.

He stepped onto dry soil and took off his mask, happy to breathe natural air again. He pulled the sunglasses out of the velcroed pouch across his chest then walked to the opening...to see hundreds of miles of Amazon jungle stretched out below him.

He was the first person in over half a century to experience the epic view.

He looked at the shallow ravine which ran downhill for sixty feet until it disappeared into the jungle foliage below. It wasn't terribly steep, but it was full of rocks and would be an awkward climb down in his dive gear, especially trying to get a foothold amongst the wet stones and flowing water.

He lifted his mask and spoke into the intercom.

"I made it out. What's your status?"

His friends didn't respond.

He frowned uneasily at the silence and looking back out at the jungle spoke again.

Suddenly Amber's voice returned, almost unrecognizable due to static.

He could only hear a few jumbled words but he understood immediately.

"Hector...caught us...guns... Roger 3..."

"Roger 3" was the code they used to tell each other to stop using and disable their intercom system. Clearly Travis and Amber were trapped, and she was alerting him to cut their communications before Hector hacked their system the same way he had the Claymires' earlier in the day.

Maddox opened his mouth to respond but suddenly paused as he saw in the distance five helicopters approaching high above the jungle a couple miles away. With a grin he pushed the button again and replied, "Sheriff in the sky. Over."

Through the static he could hear only two words from Amber.

"Copy that."

Nothing more needed to be said. Maddox quickly tapped a couple buttons on the side of the mask. Instantly a small receiver and microphone popped out of the side, and grasping them he tossed both pieces of tech back into the pool of water with the still frenzied piranha.

=================

Below Maddox in the cavern Hector and six of his men slowly circled Travis and Amber. All the mercenaries were wearing the strange underwater suits and had removed their dive helmets, all pointing spear guns at the Rebels. Hector carried a machete.

"Where is Maddox Tarver?"

When they didn't respond he ordered them to hand over their masks while telling his men, "See if you can trace his location using their intercom system."

Amber swallowed and staring back lied, "He didn't make it Hector."

Standing beside her Travis continued the act. Pointing at the black water he said, "He was killed in there. A hundred piranha."

Hector smirked disbelievingly and stepped towards the water to look closer. "Then how did you two swim out?"

Unexpectedly the monster Payara appeared at the water's surface, its two immense fangs and black eyes protruding out of the water, small pieces of the chainsaw still stuck in its mouth. The creature circled the pool's edge as if it was trying to get a look at everyone before with a flash of its tail it dove back down out of view.

Everyone leaped back from the black water in fearful shock except Hector who continued standing close to the edge as if nothing had happened. He suddenly screeched and pointed at the black water, "*NO! NO!* You two are going in there and bring out my helmet!" His frantic impatience had almost completely blinded his reason, and a stream of frothy spit spewed from his mouth with every outraged word.

A strange stillness filled the cavern as no one moved out of fear of both the Payara *and* Hector. The quiet was broken as the sound of gunshots could be faintly heard from above. Suddenly the radio strapped to Hector's shoulder crackled to life and the faded voice of one of the two injured Vultures on shore reported in a panic, "Police helicopters...we're under attack!" Hector wiped his foaming mouth across his arm and responded coldly, "Hold them off on your own. We aren't coming back till I've retrieved the treasure." He then pointed the machete at Travis and Amber then towards the dark water. "Both of you. Back in."

But then the radio crackled again and the Vulture outside reported in alarm, "We can't stop them! They've landed and are already confiscating some of the equipment!!"

A new look of horror crossed Hector's ugly face and he finally relented.

"*Everyone* back to the pier!"

==================

Above the cavern Maddox slowly examined every rock and crevice in the cave, careful to avoid stepping back into the gurgling water which was still full of piranha swimming in excited circles. With the monster "vampire" fish no longer a threat he knew the school of piranha would likely rip him to pieces if he re-entered the water.

He also knew he was going to leave the cave by climbing down the rock filled ravine to the jungle below. From there he would then try to make his way back to the swamp, hopefully to find Hector and his eight men wearing handcuffs and his friends uninjured. There was just one last thing for Maddox to do.

Find the treasured dive helmet.

He took off his sunglasses and searched every inch of the shadowy cave. Nothing. But then he noticed what appeared to be a torn piece of white cloth or bandage barely sticking out from behind a rock eight feet above the ground. Carefully he grasped a couple stones in the cave wall and pulled himself up until his head was level with the cloth.

But it wasn't a cloth or bandage. It was a strange looking military flag. Only a handful of people in the world knew what or where the flag represented. Maddox was one of those people.

He looked closer and saw that most of the flag was hidden behind a clump of jagged rocks and that it was draped over a large unusually shaped object. Securing his feet so he wouldn't fall he reached in and triumphantly lifted the flag, already knowing victory was his.

There, covered in dirt and grime but still in flawless condition, was the legendary dive helmet. With a grunt he lifted the sixty pound treasure and carefully climbed down. He then dipped the helmet into the water to clean it then lifted it up into the sunlight. Every inch of the helmet's metal was completely covered over in a thin layer of gold, and dozens of red, blue, and green jewels including white diamonds covered the faceplate and every protruding bolt. The reflection was so bright he had to put his sunglasses on to protect his eyes. The glass behind the metal frame was still covered in mud, and with a swipe from Maddox's hand fifty some years of grime was wiped away to reveal the glass was still in perfect condition as well. He had recovered over three hundred pieces of various types of treasure in the last two years, but none were as special as this.

=================

Hector and his men broke the swamp's surface, images of defeat reflecting off the glass of their dive helmets. Thirty feet in front of them four police helicopters had landed on the swamp's shore, and the wooden pier was swarming with officers carrying handguns and wearing body armour. Both of Hector's men were handcuffed and kneeling on the ground, each with gunshot wounds, while every piece of the gang's specialized dive equipment was being loaded into the helicopter's cargo holds.

And hovering above the swamp itself was the last helicopter, the officers on board pointing machine guns down at Hector and his men who were bobbing back and forth in the brownish churning water. The bearded criminal turned to dive but a stream of bullets sprayed the water ahead of him as a warning...and for the first time in his criminal career Hector put his arms into the air in defeat.

The helicopter lowered until the pontoons met the water and the mercenaries in their odd looking dive suits were pulled up at gunpoint. Their weapons were confiscated, their dive helmets were removed, and they were placed in handcuffs. All in a matter of seconds.

Travis and Amber were then pulled out of the water and worn handcuffs were also placed around their wrists. It took them five minutes to explain they were the ones who had radioed for help. Hesitantly the officers began to believe them and they were allowed to sit away from Hector and his hired men. But the handcuffs remained.

Amber immediately pulled out her tablet and began to tap the screen to trace Maddox's location using the scuba suit's built in GPS locator. Angrily the officer in charge noticed and ripped the tablet out of her hands. He then handed the computer to an associate who placed it inside a plastic bag with the penciled words *EVIDENCE* taped across. She and Travis protested and explained there was another person to save in the swamp.

"We do not have the scuba equipment senhora to conduct a search."

"Look at us, we do! Let us stay so we can help him until you return! You can't take off and leave Maddox behind!"

Officer Ortiz shook his head and replied over the engine roar, "There are no criminals left senhora to worry about. The other two thieves, a large balding man and a blonde haired woman, were picked up on the Amazon River a half hour ago." He then pointed at the other helicopters on shore which were nearly finished seizing the criminal's gear.

"No, we leave in five minutes."

==================

Maddox chuckled to himself, still half-stunned at the helmet's rare beauty and condition. He then lifted the flag into the sunlight. It was torn in a dozen places, and the colours had almost faded away completely. There were also faint dark marks across the flag, and Maddox knew it was dried blood from the *Rainforest Rogue* who had fought the monster Payara years before.

Maddox then spoke out loud as he put together the *Rogue's* mystery, "So you escaped the Bounty Hunter's "prison" by discovering the secret tunnel, somehow fought off the

"Vampire" Payara, then stored the helmet in here because you were bleeding out and couldn't carry it down into the jungle."

He then stepped to the cave's entrance and looked at the dense green vegetation at the bottom of the bubbling ravine. He then asked out loud, "But how did you survive in the jungle?"

Maddox then undid his dive tank and left it in the cave, and used the straps to instead tie the treasured helmet to his back. It would take him a while to get used to the extra weight, but he was in excellent physical shape and he could handle the sixty pounds without too much trouble. He then placed the olden flag into a waterproof pocket along his arm. Finally he pulled out the chainsaw from behind his back and thought of leaving it behind...but decided instead to keep it. He might need it when he stepped back into one of the world's most dangerous jungles below.

And then he felt the cave shudder.

He looked down and could see the piranha were suddenly swimming in all directions in hysterical alarm, and a handful even jumped clear of the water onto the sandy soil.

The cave shuddered again and Maddox could feel the rumble coming from directly below the pool of water. He pulled his dive mask off the velcro patch across his chest and turned on the goggle lights. Hesitantly he then lifted it over the dark pool and shone the light down...to reveal deep in the water the two massive fangs of the monster Payara as it tried to squeeze through the passageway and swim up into the cave!

Maddox spun away from the water but before he could take a step outside the Payara finally broke through, swimming furiously up into the cave and leaping directly at Maddox who still stood near the water's edge. All Maddox could see was a blur of one of the creature's black eyes and its white fangs as it smashed directly into his chest.

The force of the blow violently pushed him out through the cave entrance and he began tumbling down the rocky ravine towards the trees below. Unable to stop he smashed into a dozen stones sticking out of the gurgling water, and his dive mask and chainsaw were ripped away and lost. He frantically wondered what happened to the Payara just as he reached the bottom and landed painfully sideways into a larger steam.

He groaned in agony and slowly sat up in the flowing water, correctly guessing that the stream eventually fed into the Amazon River. He tried to stand but the pain was too intense and unbearable. He then slowly lifted his left leg and groaned again at what he saw. The leg had been severely smashed, and a large welt, almost the size of a baseball, had formed under his dive suit. It now looked as if he had two left kneecaps instead of one. He then checked his chest and was relieved to discover that the fish's fangs had only torn across the outside of his dive suit instead of impaling him. He then instinctively reached back and faintly grinned.

The treasured helmet was still there.

But his grin faded as he looked up and saw his copper coloured sunglasses were a half dozen feet away in the jungle grass...beside a painted human foot.

Maddox looked up as over thirty Amazon natives stepped from beyond the trees and joined the dozen who were already standing at the stream's edge looking at him. Their bodies were covered in tattoos, paint, piercings, and crude pieces of clothing made out of animal skins. He immediately recognized them as being from the same tribe he had briefly met during the motorcycle chase earlier in the day. He saw no children and suspected they were watching from the safety of the jungle vegetation.

A tense quiet followed and the only sound to be heard was the flowing waters of the stream. Maddox finally spoke a couple words in English but every native man and woman continued staring at him without blinking, their faces expressionless. He pointed at the sunglasses on shore by their feet but they paid no attention.

He felt his strength returning a little and he tried to stand again, only to drop into the flowing water for the second time. He wondered if the natives would try to help him. Instead what he saw horrified him. Three natives stepped into the water and withdrew long strange daggers and quietly approached.

In the last two months Maddox had faced death multiple times, and he had been forced to find a way to survive on his own more than once. But he had never felt as powerless and alone as he did now. He was severely injured and unable to walk, hopelessly outnumbered, and separated from Amber and Travis.

He nervously pulled himself backwards into deeper water as the natives edged closer, their expressions now deadly and frighteningly intense.

Then an idea hit him, and he wondered if he had finally figured out the last part of the mystery as to how the *Rainforest Rogue* had survived. Hurriedly he lifted one of his hands up in surrender and the native warriors hesitated. He then reached inside his dive suit and pulled out the old black and white photo he had taken from the Bounty Hunter's hideout in the

Congo a week before. With the natives watching puzzled, he unfolded the picture and handed it to the warrior who was standing nearest to him.

Nervously the warrior stepped forward and grabbed the picture out of his hand. Maddox simply grinned and pointing at the photo said, "That's the *Rainforest Rogue*. The man you helped save right here many years ago."

The warrior stared blankly at Maddox unable to understand one word. But the warrior then looked closely at the picture then hastily rushed back onto the shore calling out a name toward the trees. In a matter of moments an elderly native wearing elaborate animal skins and carrying a wooden cane for stability stepped onto the pebbles and grass of the stream bank. With respect the warrior bowed his head and pointed at Maddox before placing the picture in the shaking hands of the elderly Chief.

The Chief studied the black and white portrait for a long time and most of the natives on shore moved away from Maddox and circled the Chief to look at the picture as well. Excitedly they all began talking to one another in a language Maddox could not understand, while the Chief looked at the picture, then down at Maddox in puzzlement.

One of the women stepped away from the others and walked back towards the stream. Stopping she picked up Maddox's sunglasses and looked at her reflection in the copper tinted shades. Ignoring Maddox she then ran back towards the Chief and handed them to him. The elderly leader stared at them seemingly forever, and then he lifted a rock and scraped it against one of the sunglass's lenses. No scratch was left behind.

With a cry of joy the Chief raised his cane in celebration and yelled something which was immediately repeated by every other native. Maddox realized he had suddenly gone from an enemy to something of a hero in their eyes.

Happily the Chief quickly ordered his men to help Maddox out of the water. With their sharp knives now sheathed the same three warriors who had planned to kill Maddox before now walked back into the water to lift him out to safety as a friend.

And then the monster Payara struck again.

The creature reappeared out of the water behind Maddox and bit savagely down, its immense bottom fangs curling around the treasured helmet and straps.

Then effortlessly it lifted Maddox backwards into deeper water where it then swam furiously into the jungle before diving under the surface. With no dive mask Maddox had to simply hold his breath, and as the "Vampire" fish dragged him through the water he couldn't reach the straps behind his back to break free.

He lost track of the direction the Payara was headed and the monstrous fish left the stream and entered another body of water, this one much deeper. Maddox realized that the creature was likely carrying him away to some sort of underwater cave or nest, where he would be killed.

He gave up trying to reach for the straps and instead went for his dive knife. The pain in his body from the ravine fall was briefly gone, and unstoppable adrenaline filled his body. His hands finally grasped the knife and he tried to spin to face the creature. He then realized that the fish had already swum deep enough that there was almost no light coming through the water from above, and he would have to fight in the dark.

The Payara began cutting to the left and right, and finally one of the straps loosened. Maddox was still trapped but he could now turn his body enough to face the monster. In the dark he reached up and felt the ancient dive helmet and then one of the colossal fangs curled around it. He couldn't see anything and held on, lifted himself up and swung for the side of the fish's head.

Direct hit.

The entire blade right up to the hilt went straight through the Payara's left eye. The creature shook its head in fierce shock and Maddox lost his grip on the knife and was pushed back down. The fish seemed to have completely gone berserk, and it cut back up towards the surface and began swimming in circles before with a sharp cut of its tail it headed in a new direction.

Maddox began coughing as his lungs had almost reached their ultimate limit. His only hope now was that the Payara would somehow die and he could pull himself free in time. But the oversized underwater predator only seemed to pick up speed in the dark jungle water.

The Payara entered an underwater cavern and swam furiously to the end, where it then entered the underwater tunnel where they had first spotted the creature chasing the piranha. Hurtling forward it continued to drag Maddox through the tunnel, until it swam up into the now flooded immense cavern then down the submerged twenty foot slope until it plunged into the "jail" then through the open gate into the steamboat.

It drove forward angrily through the twisted underwater ruins of the steamboat, and a couple rusted beams struck Maddox who could only raise his arm to protect himself. The Payara finally curled through one of the cut openings in the ship's hull, and for the first time ever the monstrous fish swam into the secluded swamp.

Maddox was beginning to lose consciousness but he refused to give up, and with every ounce of strength he held his lungs in check two seconds longer. He knew the fish had taken him back to the swamp and he could only hope his friends were still there to rescue him.

But Amber and Travis were fifty feet above the water inside the police helicopter, which was turning in the sky to follow the other choppers back to police headquarters in Brazil.

As the helo spun away, Travis noticed the dark shape of the Payara shoot out of the water below and then Amber spotted Maddox. They shouted at the pilot to turn back and land. Ortiz agreed half way. He ordered the chopper to turn back and hover over the swamp, but not yet to land.

Maddox was still on his own.

After breaking the surface the confused Payara dropped back into the swamp water, swimming in another circle before turning and heading directly for the pier. As Maddox began to finally drown he realized the giant predator had gone crazy because of the blow to the head, and it was now simply swimming in any direction with no clear purpose or reason.

The Payara smashed into the now empty pier as the helicopter hovered above, and Maddox's body shot out of the water as the dive straps behind his back finally snapped. He tumbled across the rotted wood until he struck one of the pillars at the end and dropped onto the shore mud below, coughing up blood and mouthfuls of swamp water.

He simply knelt in the mud for another minute, his body trembling. The shaking subsided and he looked down at his leg, surprised that the hideous welt beneath the suit hadn't grown larger. He then wiped a clump of weeds and algae away from his eyes with a hand that was just as covered in mud. The movement caused his ribs and left shoulder to burst in shocking pain. He screamed again, but knew he was going to be okay.

The unique confident grin returned...until he reached back with his right hand and realized the helmet was missing. Turning he then noticed the pier was shaking as if it was being blown by a strong wind. Slowly he grasped the wood and began to pull himself back up onto the pier.

High above Travis and Amber were watching everything, cheering and yelling at Ortiz to take them down. But he refused.

Officer Ortiz was a brave man, one of the best officers in the entire continent of South America. But he suffered from a crippling fear of sharks and anything that could swim and bite. When he looked out the chopper window Maddox had already landed in the swamp mud out of sight behind the pier. But what Ortiz did see on the pier horrified him. Tossing the binoculars aside in a hurry he stated in a panic that "only the proper animal authorities" could handle the situation. With his voice beginning to tremble he ordered the pilot to pull away from the swamp for good.

Maddox climbed onto the pier and couldn't believe what he saw.

At the very end was the Payara with both of its hideous fangs stuck through the wood from below. The monster fish brutally shook back and forth to escape, and as the pier rattled pieces of timber began breaking free into the water. But the wooden pier still held.

Now that the Payara was in the sun Maddox could see that there were a number of jagged white scars along the creature's silver back, courtesy of the *Rainforest Rogue* from their brutal fight years before. Then Maddox saw the treasured helmet. Stuck inside the Payara's white mouth, it was wedged against the small side teeth. Some of the jewels and diamonds were gone, and portions of the gold coating had been scraped off, revealing the original brown metallic colour underneath. Unbelievably it hadn't been swallowed yet into the creature's stomach.

Far above Amber and Travis continued watching with high-powered binoculars while screaming at Ortiz to look. He ignored them and they finally gave up, focusing their attention on Maddox and the "Vampire" fish below as the helicopter began to pull away from the valley. Their anger at Ortiz quickly subsided as they realized Maddox was okay and that the Payara was stuck.

Travis chuckled as he stared at the ten foot underwater predator. "I can't believe it! It's even bigger than the scorpion was!"

He then shifted his focus to Maddox, "He'll just have to wait a couple extra hours on shore until we get back."

Amber agreed...until her expression suddenly turned uneasy.

"Travis?"

"Yeah?"

"Why isn't he leaving the pier?"

Below them Maddox hesitated as he stared at the legendary helmet. Could he really reach inside and pull the priceless object out before the Payara broke free? Was his leg now strong enough to leap in and back? He then suddenly got the feeling he was being watched, and he turned to see five painted faces staring at him through the trees lining the swamp. They were clearly members of the same tribe from the ravine...and they were too afraid of the giant fish to approach the pier.

More pieces of wood splintered into the air as the Payara shook its head with a newfound ferocity to escape while its tail turned the swamp water behind into a wild frothy mess. If he was going to try to save the helmet, he had to try now.

Maddox was not stupid. He only took risks when he had too. And reaching into one of the most frightening set of jaws in all of nature for simply another treasure was beyond stupid.

But unlike Travis and Amber, Maddox knew the treasured helmet's true secret and worth. And it had nothing to do with money.

Taking a deep breath he stumbled towards the monster fish...and leaped for the helmet.

High above his friends watched with horror and Amber screamed, "*NOOO!*"

Just then the helicopter finally lifted clear of the valley and the swamp disappeared from their view.

"Turn around! Please! Turn around! Turn around!"

Ortiz still refused. But the pilot listened, and despite Ortiz's threats of getting him fired, the pilot quickly turned the chopper around and in moments they re-entered the valley.

Amber and Travis sat on the edge of their seats in anxious panic and stared down at the jungle through their binoculars as the swamp slowly came back into their sight.

Maddox, the monster Payara, and most of the wooden pier were gone.

It was obvious that the Payara had finally broken free and dragged a mouthful of timber, and possibly Maddox, down into the water. All Travis and Amber could see were two natives standing on shore, both of them staring out at the swamp in fear. In a matter of seconds they too disappeared back into the Amazon Jungle, the water surface slowly became still again, and everything in the isolated swamp grew deathly quiet.

EPILOGUE: A REQUEST FROM INDIA

(Brazilian Coast – Remote Beach Town – 3 Weeks Later)

The nervous waiter picked up the tray and hurried across the warm sand towards the small table for two on the beach. Nervously he stopped and set the drink down beside a strange looking tablet computer as the afternoon sunlight reflected off the glass.

"Can I interest you two in-"

Amber raised her hand and almost whispered in reply, her eyes red with stress and lack of sleep. "We're fine thank you."

The waiter nodded his head politely and quickly left.

She lifted the banana cocktail and tiredly took a small sip. She then slid it back onto the table regretting she had ever ordered it. Travis didn't even bother to touch the local beer sitting in a bucket full of ice beside him. Instead he continued to stare out at the Atlantic Ocean and the small rolling waves at the edge of the beach fifty feet away. The beach was relatively quiet. There were only a few sunbathers, a couple families having a picnic, and a half dozen college age girls playing basketball on a court near the restaurant behind them. Beyond the beach and small restaurant were a couple dozen small homes and tourist shops, and beyond that a few remote dirt roads, farm land, and then the jungle.

Amber broke the quiet.

"My father called me an hour ago. He's received everything we've sent him...Wolfgang's notebook, the old safe, and he's already downloaded all the pictures from my tablet and dive mask. He'll begin studying everything with his lab equipment and he'll text me the moment he makes a discovery."

Travis finally turned to the beer.

"It won't matter much without Maddox."

When she didn't respond he continued, "I wanted Judy to meet Maddox when she wakes up back in Hawaii."

"She will Travis! And my father will get to thank him for saving his life."

A few more quiet moments passed until she spoke again.

"I thought tracking down the old jungle man would answer everything."

Travis made a sour face after trying the beer and replied even more sourly, "The old geezer knows of ten different tribes, and not one of em' ever saw Maddox. Thinks one of those un-contacted tribes must have him...maybe took him away from the swamp and the Amazon River into another part of the jungle."

He then poured the rest of the beer out onto the sand and angrily continued, "So Maddox is either fish food or trapped by some cannibals no one has ever seen. Just perfect!"

Just then a basketball from the court behind crashed into the side of Travis' chair. It was the third time in the last half hour that a basketball had "accidentally" landed near him. Sure enough, two attractive women in their twenties ran over smiling and giggling at him as they retrieved the ball. It was obvious they liked him and were trying to get his attention to ask him to join their game.

Travis didn't even turn in his chair to look. Under normal circumstances, *he* would have been the one trying to get *their* attention. But not today. Not with the heavy thought that

Maddox was likely dead. It felt to him as if everything they had achieved as a team in the last few years suddenly had been for nothing.

When he didn't respond the girls finally turned away, annoyed but determined they would try again later.

Amber watched slightly amused, then the sadness of the situation returned and she looked away and asked the same question she had asked a hundred times. The question that had no reasonable answer.

"Travis...why would he jump *towards* the Payara's open mouth?"

He continued staring at the rolling waves in a miserable daze and replied with the only answer that made any sense, "He'd only do it if he absolutely had to."

A sad silence followed as they each continued to look out at the empty ocean in quiet reflection. They had tried everything to find Maddox, and had used every contact and source they could for help. They were never going to give up, but they knew the odds of finding him in the jungle now was close to impossible. They had achieved the impossible many times before...but that had always been as a team with Maddox. For the first time in two years they both felt lost.

Suddenly the depressing silence was shattered by the deep rumbling roar from an engine's exhaust. A 16 cylinder roar.

They both turned their heads to see a black and dark purple Bugatti Chiron slowly turn off the dirt road and pull onto the hot beach sand. Smoothly and quietly the almost three million dollar, fifteen hundred horsepower hypercar drove right towards them until it stopped ten feet away from their chairs. Slowly the driver's door clicked open and a mysterious man stepped out onto the sand. With a sense of urgency he closed the door and hurriedly walked up to them.

He was East Indian, just under six feet, appeared to be in his early fifties, and had thinning black hair and a small goatee that had barely begun to gray at the edges. He was dressed in brown slacks, sandals, and a white polo shirt, while a pair of black sunglasses protected his eyes from the Brazilian sunlight. He nervously carried three newspapers under his arm, and when he took off the sunglasses to speak they could see his dark brown eyes were full of intense distress.

"I am Nihar Bombet. You are Treasure Rebels?"

Amber simply nodded her head while Travis only stared back, genuinely irritated at the man's presence. With the hypercar and expensive clothes he had Nihar pegged as a rich playboy who wanted to hire them to search for treasure so he could add some adventure to his life.

When he didn't receive the response he expected, Nihar clipped the sunglasses to his shirt and lifted the newspapers up for them to see. All three papers were from India and showed pictures of the Treasure Rebels in the news after a series of their discoveries, including when they were photographed leaving the Cairo airport roughly three months prior.

"See? I read about your famous adventures. It is honour to meet you two. My son is treasure hunter as well."

Travis stood and opened his mouth to tell the man to leave, but Amber spoke first.

"We're not accepting new members. Sorry."

Nihar shook his head in anguish and replied in his thick accent, "No, no. My son is lost in India. He went missing three weeks ago after finding special treasure underwater. He-"

Travis cut him off. "We ain't interested in bringing up your kid's treasure."

Nihar shook his head again and innocently replied, "No, the treasure is safely out of the water. That is not what I ask. I ask for the Treasure Rebels' help in finding him." He then looked at them both pleadingly and continued, "I will reward you with great knowledge. I know-"

Travis cut him off again. Something about Nihar's sincerity agitated him.

"We don't want your knowledge. You should call the police in India to find your son."

He then pointed to the papers in Nihar's hands. "And if you'd kept up with your reading you'd know we're a little busy ourselves trying to find someone." He then nodded towards the Chiron.

"Nice car...now get back in it and leave the Treasure Rebels alone."

Travis didn't wait for the man to respond. Instead he walked back to the open chair and angrily sat down to continue looking out at the ocean. Nihar turned to Amber who was still seated and looking at him. She simply said, "We hope you find your son. But my friend Travis is right. We're already busy with a life and death search of our own." She then quietly began to shift in her chair away from the Indian man to end the conversation. But before she could completely turn away he quickly exclaimed, "My knowledge is Maddox Tarver."

Their hearts seemed to stop.

Slowly and uneasily they both stood to face the mysterious man from India.

"I ask that you find my wonderful son if I provide the favour of finding for you the famous Maddox Tarver."

Travis stared at Nihar for a full three seconds. He didn't like what he saw.

"You're lying. You would be useless in a search party."

Nihar stared back coldly at Travis and intensely matched his stare.

"I am not a liar! I am a father who is willing to travel the world to hire the best to save his son! I do not intend to help find Mr. Tarver...because his location has already been discovered."

Travis and Amber looked at one another in disbelief, and then both spoke furiously at Nihar.

"By whom?"

Nihar anxiously opened one of the newspapers and lifted out a manila envelope. Realizing this was his last chance to convince them he hurriedly pulled out a glossy coloured photo and handed it to Amber.

"This was taken by a scientist travelling the Amazon River after he stepped ashore to take samples of the soil. Instead he found a small group of native men who weren't too happy to see him! He raced back to the large cruise boat he had been travelling on and sent the photo off to the authorities in Rio de Janeiro."

Travis and Amber looked at the photo which showed fifteen natives in the jungle staring at the camera as if in startled shock. Behind the natives sitting on the ground while eating food from a bowl was the blurry image of a white man wearing dark clothing.

Nihar continued triumphantly, "The photo was taken only a week ago! I spoke with this scientist and he assured me the man in the back sitting on the ground had blond hair and seemed to be healthy. That man is clearly Mr. Maddox Tarver! The coordinates of the exact location are typed out on the bottom of the picture; the scientist was very specific and accurate!"

Travis and Amber said nothing, silently studying the photo. Travis then mumbled something to Amber who nodded her head in agreement. She then handed the photo to Travis and turned away to sit back down, glaring at Nihar resentfully. The man from India looked at her incredulously, "I do not understand! Do you not want to save your-"

Travis *tore* the picture in two and shoved the pieces into Nihar's chest. The wealthy man stumbled back a couple steps and the ripped photo along with the newspapers dropped onto the warm sand.

"I tell the truth! Mr. Tarver is there!"

Travis growled, "We already searched that exact area...also a week ago."

"Then the natives are living nearby! I am cert-"

He stopped speaking as Travis stepped even closer to Nihar, looking as if he ready to punch the wealthy man from India. Which he was.

Nihar coolly stepped away then hurriedly opened the Chiron. Before stepping back in he pointed at the torn photo pieces. "That picture is genuine! My number is on the back of the picture. You call me! My son needs your help!"

With that he disappeared inside the Chiron's luxurious interior and *slammed* the car door. He punched the accelerator with his foot and spun the wheel. The hypercar flew up the beach leaving three foot high streaks of sand flying from behind the back wheels. The Chiron reached the dirt road and smoothly vanished into the distance. The small crowd which had been watching finally turned their attention away from the hypercar and the beach became quiet again.

Travis waited for the car to disappear before sitting back down, the angry pain he felt almost too much to control.

A full minute passed until Amber's curiosity got the best of her.

She stood and walked back over to the crumbled newspapers and torn photo lying on the beach. She reached down and lifted both pieces of the glossy photo free while shaking all of the sand off. She then shielded her eyes from the sun and stared intently at the picture one last time. The man in the background was just as difficult to make out as before. She then turned her attention to the natives and jungle surroundings. It was real looking enough, and the assorted tools and animal carcasses the natives were carrying looked authentic. It didn't matter, the image of the man in the background was what counted, and it still looked terribly fake.

With sadness she concluded that Travis must be right. Nihar wouldn't be the first fraudster who had tried to hire them. The picture's location was what gave it away. She let the photo fall back into the sand. They couldn't waste any time chasing false leads, especially going back to search a location they had already visited.

But then she remembered her specialized computer.

"Travis, can you bring me the tablet?"

He immediately understood what she was thinking. He felt he couldn't take any more disappointment, but he obliged her and carried the computer over.

Without another word she placed both photo fragments onto the screen and pressed a small button on the tablet's side twice. Instantly a small blue light traveled across the screen, scanning Nihar's glossy image. The tablet beeped to confirm the process was finished and she rapidly tossed the photo fragments away and tapped the screen three times. The copied image appeared on screen, enlarged and three times clearer than before.

Travis spat angrily. "Still blurry. It's photo-shopped garbage. There's nothing here that proves that's Maddox."

He then looked back at Amber, but her face was filled with hope and happiness, not disappointment.

"Look at the natives Travis! The one on the far right!"

He turned back to the digitized picture and looked intently at the last warrior, who stood confidently facing the camera. Then he saw it.

Sitting at the warrior's feet was the legendary treasured helmet, clearly visible in the enlarged image. It was brilliant. He finally turned his attention away from the treasure and back to the warrior.

And then Travis Jagson smiled for the first time in three weeks.

The warrior was wearing Maddox's sunglasses.

Travis laughed incredulously and turning his head he looked back up at the now empty jungle road, a cloud of dust from Nihar's hypercar still hanging in the air.

"I guess we're going to India after all."

Don't miss out!

Visit the website below and you can sign up to receive emails whenever Gerard Doris publishes a new book. There's no charge and no obligation.

https://books2read.com/r/B-A-WRCD-DNUO

BOOKS2READ

Connecting independent readers to independent writers.

Did you love *Amazon Swamp Victory*? Then you should read *India Yeti Pirates*[1] by Gerard Doris!

[2]

They're called Yeti Pirates. Sea robbers and hunters who claimed to have battled the famous Yeti centuries ago. Mostly forgotten, their unbelievable deeds are considered an absurd myth.

Until now, when a treasure hunter from India goes missing while looking for the Yeti Pirate's hidden loot in a Himalayan cave. The young man's desperate father turns to the Treasure Rebels for help. Owing the man a life saving favour, they rush

---

1. https://books2read.com/u/ba0dYx

2. https://books2read.com/u/ba0dYx

to India to lead the search party...unaware they're about to begin their wildest adventure yet.

"India Yeti Pirates" is the fourth adventure in the Treasure Rebels novella series, and directly follows the thrilling events of "Amazon Swamp Victory."

Read more at https://gerarddoristhrillers.com.

Also by Gerard Doris

Treasure Rebels Adventure Novella
Nile River Scorpion
Congo Spider Fangs
Amazon Swamp Victory
India Yeti Pirates
Greek Gladiator Sharks

Standalone
Wrath of the Renegades

Watch for more at https://gerarddoristhrillers.com.

About the Author

Thanks for reading! I write adventure fiction that features treasure hunters, pirates, and renegades. I'm also a fan of NFL football, westerns, classic action movies, and anything that promotes genuine adventure. For some fun updates on my writing projects, you can follow me on X (formerly Twitter) at: @gerard_advfict

Read more at https://gerarddoristhrillers.com.